STUART'S RUN TO FAITH

SHARON HAMBRICK

JOURNEY BOOKS

Greenville, South Carolina

Library of Congress Cataloging-in-Publication Data

Hambrick, Sharon.
    Stuart's run to faith / Sharon Hambrick.
      p.   cm.
    Summary: When twelve-year-old Stuart finally learns to accept
God's love for him, he changes his mind about going to school at
Greenhaven Christian Academy and living with his "preachy"
grandma.
    ISBN 1-57924-244-8 (pbk.)
    [1. Christian life—Fiction.   2. Schools—Fiction.] I. Title.
PZ7.H1755St   1999
Fic—dc21   99-11896
                                           CIP

Stuart's Run to Faith

Edited by Debbie L. Parker
Designed by Duane A. Nichols
Cover and illustrations by Del Thompson

© 1999 Journey Books
Published by Bob Jones University Press
Greenville, South Carolina 29614

ISBN 1-57924-244-8

15   14   13   12   11   10 9 8 7 6 5 4 3 2 1

To Andrew Farr

*"The fear of the Lord is the beginning of wisdom:
and the knowledge of the holy is understanding."*

Proverbs 9:10

Books in the Arby Jenkins Series

Arby Jenkins

Arby Jenkins, Mighty Mustang

Arby Jenkins, Ready to Roll

Stuart's Run to Faith

Contents

1 Dead Rats

I woke to the popping crack of the rattrap in the kitchen. It was the middle of the night, like always. Rats at my place didn't have the decency to come out during the daylight when I could whap them silly with my baseball bat or shoot them with my slingshot. No, they waited until three o'clock in the morning, when I was unconscious. They'd creep into my home through unknown passageways, nose around for food, and then—whop!—the trap would spring, snapping me back to the reality of my miserable life.

I hated those rats, but since I lived in a trailer park surrounded by tall weeds, there was nothing I could do about them. Weeds equaled rats. I had considered setting the weed field on fire, but Mom said our trailer would burn down. I'd say *good riddance* to the old heap, but Mom said to be quiet. I should be grateful that we had a place to live. Right—you try being a twelve-year-old kid cooped up in a pea-green metal box with your mom and grandma.

My name is Stuart William Baltz, known to my admirers as the Baltzman, Baltzo, or The Baltzster, but to my grandma as Stuie. Specifically, "Hey, Stuie, Baby," or some other grandmotherly address.

In any case, my mother and I lived with my grandma in a single-wide trailer because of events beyond my control.

I wouldn't mention my personal circumstances at all, except that it's "material information," as my science teacher Mr. Hogan would say. Material information is the stuff you need to know to understand a given situation. The story isn't pretty.

My dad left home when I was three months old. He never called or wrote, but I often thought about him and hoped that someday he would think about me and get in touch. I'd even asked Mom if Dad might come back some day. And I'd asked her where he was and if I could call him or visit him. For a long time she avoided answering me. She'd say things like, "You never know," or "I'm not sure, honey."

Then, one night two years ago—when Mom and I still had our own place—I couldn't sleep. I thought maybe getting something to eat would help, so I pulled on my slippers and padded silently down the hall to the kitchen. I heard a strange noise then, so I snuck back to my room, hugging the wall, and grabbed my baseball bat in case it was burglars. Peering around the corner, ready to bean any robber who had the nerve to invade my home, I saw the strange sight of my mother crying over her wedding picture album. Back then I was only ten, and maybe I didn't know very much about emotional situations, but I knew to be careful. To tread lightly.

"Hi, Mom," I said. "You okay?"

She patted the empty place next to her on the couch, meaning I should sit there. And, there in the night, my mom showed me her pictures and told me what had happened.

"In the beginning," Mom said, "everything was wonderful. I stayed home and kept the house, and Philip—your dad—worked. He had a good job at an advertising firm and made a decent living. But then the company lost a large contract, and the pressure mounted on Philip. He had to work longer hours, lots of weekends—anything to get more clients for the business."

She turned a page in her album and fingered a picture of the two of them in the back of a black limousine, leaving the wedding. They both wore smiles like sunshine, as if the world was opening up before them. As if happily-ever-aftering was just down the road and around the corner.

"Philip did not handle the extra pressure well. He started drinking. I'm afraid he became an alcoholic."

The thought of my tall, handsome dad coming home drunk scared me.

"He began to spend most of his money on his alcohol. He started staying out longer and coming home less. After a while, he didn't come home anymore."

"Do you think it was me?" I asked. Maybe if I hadn't come along, there would have been less pressure, I thought. Maybe I had cried too much. Maybe I cost too much. Maybe I—

"Don't be silly," Mom said. "A three month old is not responsible for anything. It's the adults in a situation who are supposed to be in control." Mom laughed. "Anyway," she said, reaching over and hugging me close, "that was years and years ago. We're way beyond it, you and me."

It had been ten years, maybe, but I was not beyond it. I wished I had a dad like other kids. To play ball with, and barbecue, and sit on the tailgate of a pickup truck eating sunflower seeds and spitting the shells out. And I wished my mother wouldn't cry over old pictures of other days.

"If we're way beyond it," I said, "why are we sitting here?"

Mom didn't have an answer.

Anyway, that was a couple of years ago. Right now I had the problem of the dead rat—I *hoped* he was dead—staring his eyes out a mere fifteen feet away from me. Rat Village was my secret name for our neighborhood, which

Grandma called a mobile home community, but I could tell by looking at it that this was a certified trailer park.

Mom had been sick for several weeks last year. She couldn't get out of bed, let alone go to work. By the time she was feeling well enough to get up and around, her boss had hired someone to take her place, and she was two months behind on the bills. I thought this would have been a perfect time for my dad to drop out of the sky into our lives and fix everything. But he didn't.

Things looked bad for the firm of Baltz and Son—as Mom called our family—but all was not lost. I'd overheard the conversation when Mom called Grandma.

"Mom," she'd said. "This is Patti. I've got a problem. Just how many people do you think can fit into a single wide?"

Grandma's trailer was a hideous green, but details didn't matter in a case like this. It was a last resort, a life preserver. As Mom said, "A drowning man doesn't notice the color of the rescue boat."

We'd moved here after school got out last year. My room was at one end of the trailer, right next to the living room. It was a small room, but that was not a problem since I didn't have a lot of stuff. Basically, I was a clothes-on-your-back kind of individual. I did have a few books, though, and, of course, my pride and joy—my Wheaties box collection, which didn't take up any space since it hung on the wall.

I'd been cutting off the fronts of Wheaties boxes since I was a little kid and got the idea that I'd look pretty fine with my face shining out from the Breakfast of Champions. Sort of the poor kid's answer to sports posters. Mom said she liked my Wheaties posters since they were colorful. The orange interior of my room, she said, complemented the pea-green exterior of our new home. I think she was kidding.

So, it was the middle of the night when the rattrap clattered me awake and broke the neck of a cheese-hungry rodent. I lay there wondering whether I should go ahead and take care of the hairy dead thing or wait until morning when Mom would scream, "Help, Stuart, there's a rat!" Getting up in the pitch-black to dispose of a rat was no walk in the park, but the thought of that hideous thing rotting under the sink gave me the willies.

I lay awake a long time, my thoughts wavering between my dad, long gone—moved to Chicago years ago, Mom had said—and the rat, dead under the sink.

In the morning when Mom screamed, I threw the whole thing—trap and all—over the fence into the weeds.

2 Grandma

My Grandma Ellie was a small, fluffy creature with a wrinkly face and a constant supply of chocolate chip cookies. She wore loose dresses emblazoned with large flowers, and she smelled like medicated lotion.

For years she had been an ordinary, wonderful grandma. The kind that bought you presents for Christmas, tacked your drawings up on her refrigerator, and sent five or ten dollars for your birthday. But then, about the time I turned nine years old, she made what I considered to be a big mistake, but what she believed was the greatest thing ever to happen to her, including the Reagan Administration.

"I was sitting in the chair at the beauty shop," she said, "my hair up in purple rollers and a cotton band around my head to soak up the drippings, when Jenny who does my hair invited me to come to the cantata at church. Well. . .," —she would laugh at this part of the story— "I had to say yes—I mean Jenny could have ruined what little hair I have left!"

For my part, I wished she'd gone bald and gotten it over with. But no, she went to the cantata—which is a fancy name for a choir concert—at the church here, Greenhaven Community Bible Church. This would have been perfectly fine. No problem. But the pastor had a bad habit of visiting anyone who happened to come to his church. I thought he must have too much time on his hands if he could go around doing that, but in any case, he came.

This man—Pastor Snyder—wasn't content to show up, have tea and cookies, and pass the time of day. Oh no. He had to bring his Bible and tell Grandma she was a sinner going to hell. Pretty soon, what do you know but Grandma "got saved," whatever that meant, and that was the end of the peace and quiet around Grandma's house.

She started reading the Bible, listening to sermons on the radio, and playing hymns on her organ. Hour after endless hour.

And, it wasn't good enough for her to be "saved," but she wanted us to get saved too. She said if we didn't repent of our sins and trust Christ to save our souls, we were going to fall into a real hot place called hell, where they didn't have a fire department and the flames were never put out, ever. Her stories about hell scared me. I didn't want to hear any more about it. I just wanted her to be fat and sweet and cuddly and give me five dollars.

Before we lived here, we only had to hear Grandma preach to us on holidays when we visited. But now that we'd moved here, we were live-in targets for her daily "Christianity Attacks" as I began to think of them. She saw spiritual significance in everything.

"Stuart," she would say, "didn't God make us a beautiful day today?"

If I had a good day at school, she'd say, "What a blessing," and if my day was bottom of the compost heap, she'd say, "We'll pray about it."

And it wasn't only her preaching. Grandma often played the organ at church, so naturally she had to practice at home. Her crinkly voice sang words like "bringing in the sheaves," "coming to the cross," and "everybody ought to know who Jesus is."

"He will save you," she sang. "He will save you. He will save you now." She'd look at me meaningfully, sometimes with tears pooling in her eyes.

This gave me the squirmies, I don't mind admitting it, but even this would not have been so bad if I hadn't had to go to the Christian school.

"Patricia," Grandma had said to my mom, "if you're going to live here, I simply insist that Stuart go to church and to the Christian school. I won't charge you rent, so that way you'll be able to afford the tuition."

So there it was. I was surrounded with Christians every day of the week, except some Saturdays when I got on my bike. Mom didn't mind my riding around all day, as long as I left a list of the places I'd be, and got home before dark. My list usually included these places: Mr. Watson's house, McDonald's and the library—three places a guy could relax.

Mr. Watson was the kind of grownup a kid could appreciate. He was a veteran of World War II. In fact, he'd lost an arm during that war. It always seemed strange to me that Mr. Watson had been going around without an arm for four or five decades before I was even born. I'd gotten to know Mr. Watson because he lived next door to Arby Jenkins, a friend of mine.

Actually, life at Greenhaven Christian Academy would have been unbearable if I'd had to go there without knowing anyone. Knowing Arby helped a lot, even though he and I didn't see eye-to-eye on every single issue, one of which was Christianity. The old Arbster was always after me to get saved.

"Are you a Christian yet, Stuart?" he would ask me, just about every week.

"Taking my time," I'd say. "I'm talking to Mr. Watson about it."

Part of me was just putting him on hold. On the other hand, Jenkins seemed to really care whether or not I ever got saved, and he didn't cry about it—like Grandma did—which made it easier to talk to him.

"I'm still praying for you," he'd say.

"Thanks," I would say. What can you say if someone is praying for you? Pastor Snyder says praying is "supplicating the throne of Almighty God," and a kid in my shoes couldn't have too much of that.

Other than his continual buzz about my getting saved one of these days, Arby was strung pretty tight. Little things would put him into emotional frenzies. For example, he lived with the constant apprehension that Mr. Watson was going to elope with his grandma. Still, if you've got a friend who's going to take your case all the way up to God, that's a good friend to have. Especially if you're stuck in a school like Greenhaven Christian Academy.

School quickly became a place of dread for me. Every teacher, from Mr. Kirby the Bible teacher to Coach Zeller in P.E., prayed at the beginning of class. The teacher would ask if anyone had any prayer requests. That seemed to be the signal for the kids to raise their hands and mention all the things they wanted God to give them. Some of these things surprised me.

"Pray that it doesn't rain on our field trip tomorrow," a girl might say.

One time a boy asked the teacher to pray "that we'd beat Taylor Memorial in the soccer game."

I wanted God to get me out of this school, but I never mentioned it at prayer request time.

Mr. Hogan, our science teacher, was the only teacher who didn't ask for prayer requests. And he didn't ask kids to pray out loud. He did all the praying that was to be done in that room. Maybe this was part of the reason I liked him. In other classes, I was always afraid the teacher would call on me to pray. I wanted to wear a sign that said, "I am not a Christian; do not ask me to pray."

Of course, it had to happen. Figures it would be in Mrs. McPherson's class.

Mrs. McPherson was an anomaly, an anachronism, a nonsequitur. In other words, she was out of place. What was she doing teaching at this Christian school? I never did understand it. It was one of those things my friend Raymond Sanchez called a vicissitude of life—a thing you didn't understand, might someday, but it didn't matter, because, buddy, that's the way it was.

I called her Attila the Hen. She taught English.

For one hour each day she ranted about correct usage, subject-verb agreement, and proper mechanics. I used to think mechanics was what Arby's dad, Mr. Jenkins, did at the gas station with cars. Now I knew better. Now I knew that mechanics was nouns, verbs, adjectives, and all those subordinate whatcha-ma-thingies. And Mrs. Matilda McPherson was the world's greatest living master of pulling apart a perfectly good sentence into so many pieces it needed an autopsy.

For example, one day in September stood out in my memory.

"Let's look at this sentence, class, and discuss its merits and demerits," she said.

As I listened, the blue September sky, dotted with clouds and singing with free little birds who didn't have to go to school, beckoned me outside. I sat heavily in my chair. I felt like that guy Jonah I'd heard about in chapel. The guy sat under a gourd leaf and wanted to die. I often felt like that in Mrs. McPherson's class.

Anyway, I'd studied the sentence projected on the wall. Mrs. McPherson stood poised with her ever-present red pen at the overhead projector, waiting to tear the sentence to shreds and then gloat over the remains.

The sentence was *Into every life some rain must fall.*

"Well?"

This was her discussion-starting *Well*, and I hoped someone else would come to bat for us all.

"It's a cliché," said Grace, a quiet girl who always had her nose in a book, even at lunch time, and had once announced that she wanted to grow up to be a "woman of original ideas." I thought, *such a girl!* After that I tried to flirt with her by throwing a fly with one wing on her desk. The fly spun around, uncontrolled, just like my heart at the thought of Grace. I thought that Grace, being a girl, would squeal, and I could rescue her. However, she made a fist and pounded the injured insect into her desk, and then excused herself to go wash her hands. As I said before, this was some girl.

I would have thought about Grace the whole class time, but unfortunately, Mrs. McPherson's voice had what could be called an intrusive quality. It got your attention.

"And what is a cliché?" said Mrs. McPherson. "Raymond?"

"It's a saying that is used too much," said Ray. He hated being called Raymond, but Mrs. McPherson ignored personal preferences.

"Correct, Raymond," she said. "A cliché is an overused expression that has lost its meaning. What else can be said about our sentence?"

I didn't like her assumption that the sentence belonged to all of us. Apparently no one else wanted to own the sentence either. The room was quiet. At last I decided to get it over with. Have I mentioned I don't mind stating my opinions?

"The order of words is stupid," I said, forgetting there were some things we weren't supposed to say at this school.

"Stupid?" Mrs. McPherson looked insulted, as if the moldy cliché on our wall had been her personal contribution to world literature.

"Yeah," I said.

"Yeah?"

"I mean, Yes, ma'am, stupid."

Yes, ma'am, stupid struck a number of people as funny.

"Please explain your position, Stuart."

"Well, for one thing," I said, warming to my subject, "it's dumb to start a sentence with *Into*. *Into* is a preposition, and I don't think you should start a sentence like that."

"Who agrees?" One of Mrs. McPherson's favorite tortures was to ask us who agreed or disagreed with grammatical constructions. A few people raised their hands halfway.

"I will take a stand for starting a sentence with *Into*," said Steven Adams, a pimply-faced kid who came to school in a taxi.

"You would," I said. "But I stand against it. The sentence should say, *Disaster befalls everyone*. That would shorten the sentence and make it more understandable."

"And less frothy," said Grace.

"Yes, and less frothy," I said, piercing Steven with a look, and vowing to find a way to make Grace appreciate me.

"Okay, class," said Mrs. McPherson, "it's time for a referendum. All in favor of beginning a sentence with the word *into,* please remain seated. All opposed, please stand."

This was just the sort of torment I was thinking of when I named Mrs. McPherson after the great Goth invader. Whenever she held a referendum, she made the negative position stand. That made it harder for kids to be in opposition.

I stood. Grace stood. I made a mental note to fall in love with her someday, later, when I was older. But Steven had quite a reputation for being smart. The class sat with him.

After an annoying interlude, I heard a shuffle of feet behind me. Arby Jenkins and Ray Sanchez were standing.

"Arby Jenkins." Mrs. McPherson spoke his name as if he'd won the Pulitzer Prize. "I'm surprised to see you standing. What makes you stand today?"

"I agree with Stuart," he said. His face was red, but I'll take faces in any color if they're standing by me.

"Me, too," said Ray. "Complete agreement. Stuart is right."

"Stuart is incorrect," said Mrs. McPherson. "Consider this sentence," she said, scribbling furiously on her overhead projector.

Into the mist the bloodhound nosed, scenting murder.

She tapped her pen onto the glass, making irritating little red dots like drops of blood.

"Now that," she said, "is a tremendous sentence. By beginning it with the word *Into,* I lull you into thinking the sentence is sedate and calm. Then, I sneak up on you with the *bloodhound,* and rivet you with the surprising end-word, *murder*. Who agrees?"

Hands went up around the room. I cast a look at Grace, standing across the room from me, like a lighthouse in a storm. She smiled.

"Why'd you guys stand?" I asked Arby and Ray later, when English was over and my smile-induced turbo-heartbeat had settled down to normal.

"It's personal," Arby said. "We couldn't let you stand alone." It wasn't the first time Arby had come through for me.

In any event, the *Into* incident had been back in September, when the whole fabric of Greenhaven Christian Academy was being pulled around me like a straitjacket. I was learning my first-ever Bible verses in Mr. Kirby's Bible class, singing songs I'd never imagined in chapel, and hoping the teachers would never call on me to pray.

Then one day, Mrs. McPherson did.

Jenkins sat near me in that class, and he stiffened up like a corpse when Mrs. McPherson asked me this. Jenkins knew I wasn't a Christian any more than the man in the moon was. I said, "No, ma'am," and Mrs. McPherson wasn't used to that.

"I beg your pardon?" she said.

"No, ma'am," I said. "I won't pray."

She looked at me with an expression of horror, like someone had told her she had exactly three and a half minutes to live. She sort of choked then, and I thought maybe she would have a stroke or voluntarily suffocate, which would not—I'm trying to be honest—have caused me to lose any sleep, but then she collected herself and said, "All right, class, bow your heads," and then she prayed herself. I suspect she was just saying words to get the praying part out of the way, not really "supplicating the throne of Almighty God." After that prayer, I noticed that my friend Jenkins relaxed, which is, frankly, a good thing, because take it from me, he needs to loosen up a little.

"Oh, man," Arby said to me after class, "I thought you were going to pray."

We were walking toward the auditorium for chapel. Chapel was like church at school, and we had it every Tuesday morning right before lunch.

"Not to worry, my man," I said. "I am what is called a non-pray-er."

"Good," he said. "I mean bad. I mean, come on; let's go to chapel."

Chapel that day gave me the creeps. They sang a whole bunch of songs about blood. One was,

What can wash away my sins?

Nothing but the blood of Jesus.

What can make me whole again?

Nothing but the blood of Jesus.

Another song said,

Would you be free from your burden of sin?

There's power in the blood!

And another, the worst one,

There is a fountain filled with blood

Drawn from Immanuel's veins.

And sinners plunged beneath that flood

Lose all their guilty stains.

I looked around the auditorium while these bloody songs were being sung. People sang loud and cheerfully or dull and listlessly, but no one seemed to be horrified by the words they were singing. Who wanted to be plunged into blood drawn out of somebody's veins? I was stunned, but it didn't seem to bother anyone else. Except Miss Ward, our history teacher. She had tears running down her face.

The principal, Mr. T., got up to speak. Naturally, his subject was the Blood of Christ.

"The Bible tells us," he said, "that there can be no forgiveness of sin unless blood has been shed."

I tuned him out and thought about Grace.

3 Coach Pickering

Chapel was held every Tuesday, but our other all-school get-together was on Friday. Every Friday afternoon we had a pep rally. A pep rally consisted of the whole student body, from seventh to twelfth grades, cramming into the bleachers out on the soccer field. The cheerleaders would jump around in their green and white outfits, doing a few yells that centered on the shout, "GCA! GCA! GREEEEEN-HAVEN!!!"

After the cheers, the vice-principal would get up and shout into the microphone that we were now going to find out which class had the most school spirit.

Rex Whitney, the senior class president, ran to the microphone first.

"Okay, seniors!" He shouted as if there was not a microphone two millimeters from his lips. "Let's show all these younger kids who's in charge here!!!"

All the twelfth graders stood up and screamed, "GREEEENHAVEN" over and over. Each grade did this, down to the worms of the school, the seventh graders. Our president was a girl named Katy, but never mind her being a girl; she could scream into a microphone just fine.

As the seventh graders rose around me screaming, I wondered why they wouldn't stand up in class for a fellow student, yet they would stand out in the open air screaming "GCA, GCA" like they were going to get a prize for knowing the letters.

The pep rally surged around me, but my mind was elsewhere. Grandma had awakened me that morning by playing her organ. Lying in bed, looking around my walls at my Wheaties-box posters—knowing I *could too* get my picture on one someday if I had some decent coaching at my running—listening to Grandma bringing in the sheaves, I had wondered how I might be able to earn some extra money. Then Mom and I could get our own private home again and have some peace and quiet in the morning.

I flipped through the basic money-earning options in my mind—paper routes, lawn mowing, baby-sitting—when the word *running* slapped me out of my reverie and back to the pep rally. If there was anything in the world I could do, it was run.

"Anyone interested, please show up after school Monday. Three o'clock sharp."

"What, what?" I said to the kid beside me on the bleachers.

"Junior high cross-country practice," he said. "Weren't you listening?"

"Cross-country practice?" I said.

"Yep. Three o'clock. Do you run?"

"Yes," I said. "I run."

"So be there," he said.

I could run forever, and in fact, it was a serious plan of mine to acquire superior training so that I could break all existing college records in both short- and long-distance races. I would then advance to the Olympics, where I would blast away all competition and become the gold medalist in eight events. Then I would be able to support my mom in style. Fancy house, swimming pool, housekeeper, Rolls Royce—the whole deal.

And maybe, if I were a famous runner, my dad would see me on television, or even see my face on a box of Wheaties and think to call me up. Maybe.

When Monday afternoon came, I was there, trotting up and down the field, trying to stay loose, waiting for whoever the coach was to come out and tell us to run a lap or two to see what we were made of.

At last, a tall, gangly individual in a derby hat—the kind they used to wear back in the fifties when everybody had a dad at home—appeared and said, "Junior high cross-country, over here."

I had never seen this man before, but I trotted over. Maybe he was a parent who'd been asked by Mr. Thompson to let us know the coach wouldn't be there and we should all go home for the day.

"My name is Sydney Pickering," he said, "but don't blame me. My parents named me in a fit of confusion. If you'll call me Coach, that would be just fine, got it?"

"Sure, Coach," a bunch of guys said. But I thought, "Sydney! Why did he even tell us that?"

I also thought that with such a yahoo as this coaching the cross-country runners, I was never going to be challenged. He probably couldn't even run and would confine his coaching to telling us to run a large number of laps while he sat on the bleachers reading the *Wall Street Journal*. This disappointing scenario meant I would have to wait to get started on my serious running. The Olympics seemed distant, the Wheaties box unreachable.

There was one consolation. Even with a so-so coach, at least this would be one school activity that wouldn't be dripping with all that God stuff.

Which shows how much I knew. Leave it to a guy named Sydney to make running into a Christian exercise.

"I've chosen Philippians two, verses three through eighteen as our team verses this year. Everyone will have these memorized within two weeks, got it?"

"Got it."

Then Sydney "the killjoy" Pickering read those sixteen long verses to us, and then he prayed, but I didn't pay any attention. He then stripped down to his athletic clothes, which I couldn't believe he wore underneath his outside clothes instead of just bringing them in a gym bag and changing.

"Follow me."

I guessed he might last a couple of laps, a mile at the most. Which shows that I hadn't yet gotten to know "Pickering the Indomitable," as I called him later.

He led us on a route I dubbed the "Circuit of Torture." Up hills, through streams, right past my trailer park. Thankfully my Grandma was nowhere to be seen. I was embarrassed about living there and had kept it a secret from everyone. Even Arby and Ray didn't know where I lived. If we got together out of school time, I always went over to their neighborhood. Mostly we hung out together at Mr. Watson's house. In any event, I didn't want people to know I lived in such a pigsty of a place. And if my grandma had, at the moment we ran by, come out and seen me, she would have waved a dishtowel and squealed, "Stuie, Stuie! Hi, Baby!" And this would have caused me a number of problems which I do not wish to discuss.

When we finally made it back to school—sweating rivers, gulping oxygen—Pickering led us through some bleacher runs before we knocked off for the day. Half the guys quit the team at the end of the first practice, and one kid—what a loser—stopped halfway through the Torture Route and called his mom from a pay phone to come pick him up.

I heard about it the next day because I had been up front, right behind Pickering. Because, as I've said, if there's anything I can do, it's run.

I was sweating like a mad dog when practice was over, but it felt good.

"Okay, guys," Pickering said, "that'll do for a beginning. We'll see if we can turn that up a notch tomorrow. If you're still game, show up at three o'clock. And now," he said, "if you'll excuse me, I have to go work out."

Now here was a man I could respect. In spite of his Bible verses and long prayers.

4 Hogan the Cool

One time I read about one of the Russian czars, a deranged maniac who ruled Russia like it was a slug and he was the saltshaker. His name was Ivan the Terrible, and I didn't blame them for calling him that. Lots of English kings had nicknames, too, like William the Conqueror, Edward the Confessor, and Edgar the Peaceful. I mention these men because one night when I couldn't sleep I was thinking of them, and my mind slipped into thinking about some of the people I'd met since we'd moved to Greenhaven and what they might be called if they were kings.

I thought of Mr. Watson first. His name was easy: *Watson the Kind.* I had a real soft spot in my heart for Mr. Watson because he had come out of nowhere to be nice to me when I didn't deserve it. I had actually stolen money from him, and yet he was good to me and took me on a Father-Son retreat with the church men's group. There was no reason for him to take me, except to be nice. And the way he invited me had made me feel like I would be doing him a favor by going.

Mr. Watson always prayed for me to become a Christian, and at the retreat, when I had questions about the sermon, he answered them, but he didn't pressure me. He would answer my questions about my Bible class or chapel, but he didn't push me. One time I asked him why.

"How come you never ask me to Accept-the-Lord-Jesus-as-my-Savior-right-now?"

"Because you are not under conviction for your sins, and you don't yet see your need of a Savior, which by the way, is very real and very great."

"Oh." His answer had startled me.

"But when you are ready to commit your life to Christ, I would be happy and honored to pray with you."

"Uh, thanks, Mr. Watson," I said, "maybe someday."

After several cross-country practices, in which I could feel myself becoming stronger, I knew I needed a name for Coach Pick that indicated strength and endurance. *The Indomitable* was the name I finally settled on because I'd seen it written under a picture of Sir Edmund Hillary, the leader of the first group of men to get to the top of Mount Everest. I figured if he could climb to the peak of the highest mountain in the world, then he was good enough to be in company with Sydney Pickering.

The third person I named was Mr. Hogan, my science teacher. Hogan was hands-down the best teacher at GCA, though he scared us all—even me—sometimes. I called him *Hogan the Cool* because he always spoke in flat-out realities. He didn't mess around.

He gave difficult assignments and made us think things out. At first I thought he'd go easy on me because I was a new kid at this school, and I didn't have a dad around like most of the other kids did. However, that kind of copping out didn't fly with Hogan the Cool. Hogan didn't accept excuses from anybody.

For example, several weeks ago—back at the beginning of the school year when I didn't know Mr. Hogan very well—I was daydreaming in science, completely checked out for the class period. I was remembering a funky Japanese film I'd seen once in which a crazed scientist throws vials of an overpowering growth hormone into a town's water supply.

Well, the reservoir was populated with little frogs. So, the teeny little frogs get ahold of micrograms of supersynthetic growth hormone and, you've got it, they grow. They grow and grow and grow into huge monstrous frogs that tower over all the buildings. These frogs then pad down the streets—galomph, galomph—belching dynamite *ribbets* that cause numberless people to up and die of fright.

Screaming and running about reach epic proportions, and the whole town is in hysterics, except one steady-tempered, middle-aged professor in black-framed glasses who figures the frogs won't be able to get enough to eat. Right enough, after five or six horrifying days the frogs begin to die, crashing over in pathetic flops, crushing buildings, trains, and slow-moving people. Then this town has to figure out how to get rid of these rotting, stinking frog carcasses, and . . .

It was at that moment in my daydream that I was startled by the absolute silence around me. Mr. Hogan was standing over me, staring down at me, fingering his map pointer.

"Mr. Baltz," Mr. Hogan said, "the meaning of fission please?"

"Don't know," I said.

"Don't know?"

"Don't know, sir," I said.

"And what, may I ask, have you been thinking about during the last fifteen-minute discussion of fission and fusion?"

"Frogs," I said, figuring I could get a laugh. No one laughed.

"I see." And he stared into my very soul, and I felt a little bit—just a tiny bit—guilty or something for not having listened to him.

I'd had to stay after class for the predictable Talk that Hogan always had with kids who didn't cut the mustard in his class.

"Frogs, Mr. Baltz?"

"It was a movie," I said. "You know, one of those cheap Japanese movies from the sixties."

"I do not know."

"Oh," I said.

"Any reason you can't stay focused on class?"

I thought of all kinds of reasons that might have worked with the psychologist at my old school—like that I hated my life and my grandma's organ playing and the potholes and rats and having to hang around religiously fixated people—but of course none of this would have counted with Hogan, the world's greatest living master of chopping up excuses into dog meat.

"Nope."

"Nope?"

"No, sir."

Hogan and I sat there for a while—Mr. Hogan, I mean—and then he did a big thing. A really big thing. That he didn't need to do in a million billion years.

"When I was a kid," Mr. Hogan said, "my father left home."

I looked at the floor. "Oh," I said.

"So I often felt like I wasn't as good as the other kids whose fathers had not left."

"Oh," I said. So he could read minds too.

"And also that I didn't have to perform up to their level."

I stared at a crack in the floor.

"Look at me, Stuart," he said, using my first name for the first time.

I looked up, forcing myself to hold his laser-beam gaze.

"I said, I also thought that because my home was disadvantaged without a father that I didn't have to perform up to the level of the other students."

I looked down again.

"Look at me."

I looked.

"Is this your belief, Baltz? That you don't have to pay attention in class? That the only thing you can do is run? That you don't have to push yourself to succeed academically?"

"I don't know," I said.

"Because," he said slowly, "if that is your belief," his voice got slower and quieter, "then I have no respect—absolutely zero respect—for you as an individual."

The effect of this was like an electric charge to my heart.

I said, "Yes, sir," man-to-man. He had hit a bull's-eye.

5 Infractions

Mrs. Matilda McPherson (the Ugly) (the Horrible) (the Inconsequential) continued to be someone I never wanted to see again, every single day of my life. When I saw her I wished I hadn't, and when I wasn't around her I hoped I never would be.

I'd pegged Mrs. McPherson as approximately one hundred and forty years of age, but perhaps she only looked it.

I had to admit her job was not an easy one. Teaching English, after all, must be the worst job in the world. For example, there's Shakespeare. William Shakespeare wrote plays four hundred years ago—before people spoke actual English. This made his plays difficult to understand. Why we had to read sixteenth-century plays aloud in the twenty-first century was a thing I could not comprehend.

"If we read them silently, we'd fall asleep," Steven Adams said.

"Good point, Adams," I said. For once I agreed with him.

Mrs. McPherson would choose a student to read. The person would read one line, maybe two, peppered with words like *Anon, me thinks,* and *Why you, Brutus?* Then Mrs. McPherson would interrupt to explain what Mr. Shakespeare meant. This went on line after line, page after page. Somehow this method of line-by-line interpretation was supposed to make us want to go to plays in which men wore tights.

The other half of English class was spent studying things we already knew. For instance, nouns. I learned nouns in second grade, and in third grade, and in fourth grade, but Mrs. McPherson thought we did not know what nouns were. Like person, place, thing is a tough concept.

But the worst thing about Mrs. McPherson was Grammar Infractions, the worst torment in her arsenal.

"Tonight I want you to play Grammar Infractions," she would say, and this was the only time I would notice the glint of human enjoyment on her face. She loved Grammar Infractions, and she would assign us to "play it" at least once a week.

The rule was you had to write down when someone made a mistake in his grammar. And then bring in a list of at least ten errors in speech you had overheard. Kids would read their lists and everyone would laugh. Except me. I thought it was rude.

One day, a girl whipped out her paper and said, "I was at the grocery store and a woman said, 'No I ain't gonna buy you no toy' to her kid." The girl smiled like she'd just won the Miss America title, but I snorted out loud like the disgusted person I was.

Snorting did not sit well with Mrs. McPherson, who asked me why I felt the need to express myself nasally.

"What happened in English class, Stuart?" said Mr. Thompson.

I was sitting in a soft blue chair in Mr. Thompson's office. I appreciated this chair after sitting all day in hard chairs specifically designed to keep kids awake in boring classes. I looked past Mr. Thompson to his large windows that overlooked the street. Cars sped past, oblivious to my predicament. A pair of antlers hung on the wall, and a large flowering cactus crouched on the bookshelf.

"Stuart?"

"I said that I thought Grammar Infractions was a rude game."

"And why is that?" said Mr. Thompson. He did not seem angry.

"It forces kids to make fun of other people." I paused, then launched into it. "And since this is a Christian school, I don't think she should tell us to make fun of people. Maybe other people don't know grammar. Or maybe their culture is different. Or maybe they don't give a rip about grammar. Maybe grammar is not the A-number one thing they are thinking about right at the moment. People should be allowed to go to the grocery store without GCA kids tattling on them to Mrs. McPherson."

"But what did you say to Mrs. McPherson?"

I wondered what would happen to Mom and me if I got thrown out of GCA. Grandma had been very clear that if we were going to live at her house, I had to attend this specific school. If I got expelled for disrespecting Mrs. McPherson, would we be homeless? Maybe Mr. Watson (the Kind) would let Mom and me live in his basement.

"What did you say, Stuart?" Mr. Thompson interrupted my thoughts of getting expelled from school.

"I said, 'What a stupid game, as if everyone knows perfect grammar.' "

"And then?"

"And then she said, 'I beg your pardon?' " I didn't tell Mr. Thompson that her face got red and her eyes blazed when she said it.

"And then?"

"And so then I said, 'Look, Mrs. McPherson, this game is mean and if you're such a great Christian, you shouldn't teach us to ridicule people.' " Evidently, this was not something I should have said to Mrs. McPherson.

"Oh," said Mr. Thompson, "I see. But since you're not a great Christian, it's okay for you to show disrespect for your teachers?"

That surprised me. I replayed in my mind what he'd said.

Mr. Thompson went on.

"Hear me well, Stuart. You know you are here on probation. We don't usually accept students who are not born-again believers in Christ. This is a Christian school, and we aim to train Christian students to serve the Lord Jesus. We accepted you solely because your grandmother begged us to."

I nodded. This was not news to me.

"So while you're here—however long that may be—"

He paused to let that threatening line sink in.

"You will obey the rules whether or not you agree with them, respect the staff whether or not you like them, conduct yourself in an orderly manner, and be decently behaved. Am I understood?"

I sat back in his chair and rested my elbows on the armrests. I fixed my gaze on his left ear and pondered for a few seconds before I spoke.

"So you want me to go around pretending I am a Christian? Wouldn't that be what you call hypocrisy?"

We'd had a chapel message recently on the "dangers of hypocrisy." Hypocrisy, Pastor Snyder had told us, was pretending to be something you're not. I always thought this was called lying, but *hypocrisy* is a big word for it.

"Did I say that, Mr. Baltz?" Mr. Thompson rose out of his chair in a way that scared me and walked around to the front of his desk. He stood in front of me, tall and menacing, and looked at me hard.

"Did I say anything that could be interpreted as meaning that I wanted you to pretend you were a follower of Jesus Christ when in fact you are not? Did I mention that you ought to pray in class, for instance?"

"No, sir."

"Did I ask you to go out on our weekend ministry teams and share the gospel?"

"No, sir."

"Did I in fact ask you to do anything other than what a normal, decent, upstanding American kid ought to do while he's in school?"

"No, sir."

"Then it's a deal," he said. "You'll behave yourself." Here he smiled. "And I won't throw you out of school."

He stuck out his hand.

I shook it.

In a sort of dream I wandered back to class, sat down, and stared at Mrs. McPherson like she was an alien life form.

The next day she announced that Grammar Infractions was hereby abolished as being disrespectful to the human race.

"Just do not say 'ain't' when I am around," she said.

6 Needing a Savior

"Mom," I said, "are you a Christian?"

Mom and I were eating shrimp and fries out of plastic, paper-lined baskets at Cook's Seafood Landing where Mom waited tables. I would go to Cook's some nights when I didn't have too much homework. During her dinner break, Mom would eat shrimp with me. Sometimes, even when I did have a lot of homework, or if I just wanted to get out of the trailer, I would go to Cook's and do my homework in a booth.

Mr. Faladini, the owner, would bring me soda pop and try to look over my shoulder at what I was doing. Mr. Faladini liked me, and he let me have all the soda I wanted and even his famous fried shrimp if I didn't make a complete pig of myself.

"Shrimp is my lifeblood, so don't drink me dry," he would say.

"I try to be good," Mom said, answering my question. "I expect that if I try to be good, that'll sit well enough with God to make things okay." She dipped a shrimp in tartar sauce, then munched it, tail and all. "What makes you ask such a thing?"

"Just wondering," I said.

I was glad it was just Mom and me having dinner together, without Grandma talking endlessly and wondering about every detail of my day.

I chowed down on Faladini's lifeblood and tried to line up the opposing teams. On one side there was Mom saying she was good enough, and on the other side was Mr. Thompson saying that being good didn't have anything to do with being a Christian, any more than it had to do with being a decent American.

"My principal says being good just makes you good; it doesn't make you a Christian. Evidently there's a lot of things you have to believe to be a Christian."

"Such as?"

"Such as—" I took a long sip through my straw and tried to sort out what I'd been learning about Christianity over the past few months.

"Well, for one thing, you have to be sorry for your sins. And for another thing, you have to believe in Jesus Christ."

"What about Him?"

"Well, for one thing, He died on a cross."

"Everyone dies," said Mom.

"And then He came back to life, and people who believe it can go to heaven." I thought that was right, but I wasn't sure. It sounded strange coming from me.

"Whatever," said Mom. "Sounds like something your grandma would say. I don't really listen."

"I have to," I said. "I get tested on it in school." I pushed the green basket of shrimp away from me.

"It won't be for long," said Mom. "As soon as I've saved enough to get us our own place, you can go back to public school. Right now Grandma insists I send you to Greenhaven Christian, and since tuition is cheaper than rent somewhere else, I go along. But don't worry. We'll get out of Grandma's place soon enough."

"Good," I said. "Then I can get back to reality."

"You and me both," she said. "I can't wait to get out of there."

"Mom!"

Mom laughed and reached over to grab one of my shrimp.

"I'm thirty-nine years old," she said. "And I have a twelve-year-old son. The firm of Baltz and Son needs its own elbowroom, you know? But don't worry, Stuart, it won't be long. I'm saving money every paycheck."

The days were short this time of year, so it was dark when I rode up to Mr. Watson's house. I rang the doorbell three times, which is my signature ring. Minutes later Mr. Watson and I were sipping hot decaf out of mugs in his kitchen. This was the usual way of things at Mr. Watson's, and I appreciated knowing that with Mr. Watson things would always be the way they always were.

"What brings you here so late at night, Stuart?"

"I have some questions."

"Go ahead," he said. "Ask away."

I sipped hot decaf like a man even though it burned my tongue. Then I thought that was stupid, and I reached for the cream to try to tame the heat.

"Tell me again about being a Christian," I said.

"Why?" he said. "What's up?"

"I told the principal that he wanted me to pretend I was a Christian, but he said no, he just wanted me to be good. And then Mom said she was good enough to be a Christian, and I wanted to tell her there was something more about being a Christian than being good. So I mentioned about

Jesus Christ dying and coming back to life, and she said, 'Whatever.' "

Mr. Watson pulled his Scrabble game off a shelf and set out the board. I lined my seven letters up and mentally steeled myself for a cutthroat Scrabble competition which I would inevitably lose. Mr. Watson was a grand champion of this game. Last time we'd played, he used all seven of his letters in one move to connect three words and form the new word *effervesces.*

"Why were you in the principal's office, Stuart?"

Oh, why had I mentioned that? I wanted Mr. Watson to think I was good because why should he let a hoodlum and expelled kid burst into his house in the middle of the night to drink coffee and play word games?

"I disrespected Mrs. McPherson." I laid down three tiles to form the word *sin*, the sort of puny word I usually started with, and waited for Mr. Watson to slam me with a seven-letter wonder.

"Ah," he said, laying all seven tiles across my *s* to form the word *salvific*. I'd look it up later, I decided. I had real things to talk about now.

"But then I had that talk with Mr. Thompson. He made me think some things through."

"Such as?"

"Such as it's no excuse to behave badly just because I'm not a Christian. I should still behave myself." I reached into the letter bag and pulled out unusable letters. It didn't look good for my team. I spelled *grace* on the board, hoping Mr. Watson wouldn't slam me for the proper noun like he usually did.

"Grace, 'tis a charming sound, 'tis music to my ears," he sang, and I wondered how he knew about Grace. I hadn't mentioned her.

He laid down *redeemer* off the *r* in *Grace,* then poured himself another cup of coffee, and grabbed more tiles from the letter bag. I hoped he'd get some lousy letters so I'd have a chance for once. "The thing is, Stuart," he said, "I pray every day that the Lord will show you your need of the Savior."

"Uh huh," I said. We'd had this talk before, and when it started to get personal like this, I was polite but tried to change the subject. Still the phrase "need of the Savior" had come up twice today. And, I'd felt sort of silly trying to explain it to Mom and being tongue-tied and unable to make sense. So I stepped out with another question, while attaching the word *effort*—my best word yet—onto the *r* at the end of *redeemer.*

"Mr. Watson," I said, knowing I was going too far for my own religious comfort," what exactly do you mean by 'need of the Savior'?"

Mr. Watson looked at the clock. Somehow it had gotten to be nine o'clock. Decaf and Scrabble will do that. Rather late for a school night. I could see the cogs of his mind whirling away: Should he keep me up too late just to answer my questions? Or should he send me home without answers in order to meet curfew? I heard him mumble, "Duties never conflict," which sounded like something Mr. Hogan would say.

"Stuart," he said, "I need to make a phone call."

Calling my mom, I guessed. When he came back, his face seemed strained.

"Here's the plan," he said, "you come over here right after track practice tomorrow. I'll feed you dinner, and we'll have a good long talk about your need of Christ. Got it?"

"Sure," I said, "it's a deal."

He swept the letter tiles into the bag and folded up the game board.

"Just don't ride out in front of a truck on the way home," he said.

"Why's that?"

"Because if you do, you'll die. And not being saved as you are, dying would be a bad case."

"Meaning?"

"Meaning you'd go to hell."

I rode home very carefully, checked my bed for poisonous snakes, and slept with my nightlight plugged in and my baseball bat handy to beat off murderers.

7 Words and Meanings

I woke up the next morning with a sore throat to beat the band. Grandma said it came from not getting home until almost nine-thirty, which was not a civilized time for a kid twelve years old to be out wandering the streets.

I wanted to defend myself by telling her I had not been wandering the streets, but had been furthering my religious education. That would have made her happy. Unfortunately, I was unable to say anything.

Mom was worried that it might be strep throat, which is a bad infection that requires antibiotics. That means a visit to the doctor and an expensive prescription. Plus I'd have to miss a day of school, and of course, I wouldn't be able to see Mr. Watson.

I wondered if a person could die of strep throat.

Mom and Grandma argued about the need for a visit to the doctor.

"Your boss should provide you with health insurance, Honey," Grandma said.

"Tell him that," Mom said. "But the fact is, he doesn't, so it's fifty bucks to see the doctor, plus the lab fee to check Stuart's throat culture, plus the medicine to clear it up. As if I am made of dollars."

I had four dollars and thirty-five cents in my old rocket bank. I pounded my pillow and thought what a drain I was on my mom. It was maddening to be only twelve years old and not be able to help out. Someday—when my face was on the Wheaties box—I would make things easy for Mom. Someday my mom would not live in a trashy single-wide and would have doctors and specialists of all kinds at her beck and call, never mind the insurance.

"Would it be all right," Grandma finally said in a very soft voice, "if I paid for the doctor visit?"

"I'll pay you back," said Mom.

It was strep. I had to stay out of school that day, and I had to take amoxycillin for ten days. It would be bad, the doctor said, if I stopped taking the medicine when I felt better. No, I had to take all the pills, and it would take a week and a half.

"The thing is," he said, "if you don't take all the pills for the full ten days, then the nasty critters don't all die. The ones that are strong can resist the drug for several days. So if you stop taking it before they're all dead, the strong ones survive."

Not a cheerful thought.

"Yes, and this is doubly bad if you pass them on to someone else. They are worse and harder to kill next time. And, you know, of course, that they multiply at a rather alarming rate."

Not to worry. I'd take all my medicine. At this point in my life, when I was afraid I might die and fall into hell, I was not going to take any chances with drug-resistant *streptococcic* colonies cavorting around in my throat.

On Monday, Coach Pickering wouldn't let me run cross-country. He said I was in "recovery mode" and therefore on the sick-and-injured list.

"You can sit on the bleachers and work on your Philippians passage," he said.

I'd forgotten about that. "Okay," I said. I was aching to run, but the primary rule of teams is this: *Obey the coach.* Obeying coaches makes them trust and respect you. I had learned this way back in second grade Little League. Like nouns. Learn it once, and it's with you.

So I sat on the bleachers under a good bunch of cumulus clouds and began with Philippians two, verse three:

Let nothing be done through strife or vainglory; but in lowliness of mind let each esteem other better than themselves.

Sometimes I had heard kids in Bible class talk about how hard the Bible is to understand, which I don't really get because it's in English, unlike Shakespeare. Take this verse, Philippians 2:3. It was easy. It meant that people should not pick fights or be full of themselves. And also that people should not think they are better than other people.

I read the verse out loud a few times because when you're memorizing it's helpful to hear the words. Then I said it to myself silently a few times. Bad mistake, because my mind wandered around to lots of people that I think I am better than.

Take Mrs. McPherson for example. Almost anyone—except perhaps Ivan the Terrible or Vlad the Impaler (who spiked his dead enemies on spears to scare off intruders)—was better than her. Although lately, since she'd dumped Grammar Infractions, she was not so repulsive.

And take, for instance, my dad. What kind of a human being was he to leave his family and then never say "sorry," never show up, never send any money, never call to say "Happy Birthday"? I knew I was in bad emotional waters to be thinking about my dad while I was supposed to be learning a Bible verse.

And why did I have to go on and on and on thinking about him? He was not going to show up, and if he did, I was honor-bound, on account of the way he'd treated my mom, to punch his lights out.

I shook myself back to reality and stared at the poofy cumulus clouds going up into forever. And there I was, one lone seventh grade cross-country kid, plunked out of practice onto the bleachers to memorize a bunch of Bible verses. Why should I memorize the Bible anyway?

Oops. Pull it together, Baltz, I thought. Remember Mr. Thompson's talk. Behave yourself and do as you're told. Obey the coach. Be a decent American.

It took the team a long time to run six miles. So verse three was a done deal long before they returned. I started in on verse four:

Look not every man on his own things, but every man also on the things of others. That one was easy, so I went on: *Let this mind be in you, which was also in Christ Jesus:*

Verse five bothered me. How could the mind of Christ Jesus be in me? Why would I want it to?

The guys finally gasped onto the field and headed for the locker room for team prayer. Coach Pickering insisted on prayer before and after practice. I ran over and caught up to Steven. Since he was so smart, I figured he'd be able to help me out.

"Steven," I said. "Who is Jesus Christ anyway?"

"What?" said Steven.

"You heard me," I said.

"Jesus?" he said.

"Yeah, Jesus," I said.

"He's the Lord," said Steven.

"Meaning what?" I said.

Steven stopped and stared at me like I was a new variety of fruit.

"I don't know," he said at last. "You just ask Him into your heart, and then you go to heaven."

"And what does that mean, anyway?" I said. "My heart is a pumping muscle. No one will fit in it."

"What?" Adams must've thought I was nuts, but the feeling was mutual at the moment.

"Ask Jesus into your heart. What in the world does that mean?"

"That's what you do to go to heaven."

"But what does it mean?"

"You just pray," he said.

I rode my bike home in a dismal mood. The one kid I asked about Jesus Christ didn't know two plus two about his own religion! I rode right past my trailer park, lost in thought.

It must mean something, I thought. Asking Jesus into your heart. Whole schools are built around this. Whole countries. People have lived and died for this. It must mean something.

I had missed my appointment with Mr. Watson because of my illness, but he'd called to see if I could reschedule for Thursday, right after cross-country practice.

"Sure," I said. "I can be there."

"Good," Mr. Watson said, "because I happen to be making chocolate chip cookies."

"Ah," I said. Mr. Watson's chocolate chip cookies are to die for. I mean, they're great. Dying was not a thing I wanted to think about, even if it was just a saying. "I'll be there for sure."

Where Mr. Watson was, there were answers, and I needed one. There was something I needed to know that Steven Adams did not know. *Who was Jesus Christ, anyway?*

8 The Pack

Coach Pick let me run on Wednesday. It was a hard run over the usual course. Around the block, down the hill, past a bunch of housing developments, past the cemetery out at the city limits, and then back around again to school. That put the hard part, the hill, at the very end. It was a slow incline, but fairly long, and since it came at the end of six miles, it was a killer.

I liked it. It made me feel strong, and I liked knowing what my body could do. My face would get really hot, and I'd sweat like a pig, or like a horse, rather. Pigs don't sweat. Instead they cover up in the mud all day to stay cool.

On Thursday Coach called me aside before practice.

"I want you to lead the pack today, Baltz. I'll be right behind you."

"Yes, sir," I said. My face smiled only a little, but inside I was having a major celebration. *Yes! Lead the pack! Breakfast of Champions, here I come!*

"Set a good pace."

"Yes, sir."

I set a strong pace, just a little bit—not much—faster than what Coach usually did. I knew I could open it up and cruise in a higher gear—now that I was used to the course— but I knew that Coach knew that too, and it's stupid to show off. It makes people despise you, and frankly, I had enough trouble in my life without people hating me for running fast. Being in front was enough for me.

"Showoff," I heard some guy say behind me. But too bad for him. If he wanted to be good enough to lead, then he should run more.

Running gave me a chance to think through the stuff that had accumulated in my mind over the last few weeks. First, school. That horrible place I was confined to for six or eight hours every day with only short happy interludes, like Mr. Hogan's science class and cross-country.

Second, home. Mom and I, we needed our own place. Living in a single-wide trailer was like living in a station wagon. Hardly any privacy. Hardly any quiet. My only escape there was to hide out in my room with my books and my thoughts.

Third, Mr. Watson and that strange idea about needing a Savior. For what? Why?

"Crank it up a bit, Baltz," Coach said, interrupting my thoughts. "You're slacking off."

"Sorry," I said. I hadn't realized I was slowing down. I torqued it up a notch as we passed the cemetery. It was uphill from there back to school.

"Well run," said Coach.

"Thanks, Coach."

We gathered together, stinking and sweating, in the locker room to pray. Coach thanked God for the good weather and that nobody got hurt on the run. He asked God to take care of us on our way home and to help us be decent adolescent individuals. He asked God a number of other things which I didn't hear because I was thinking about how good it felt to run at the front of the line. Maybe Coach would let me lead the guys all year. Yes, I was that good.

My shower felt good, washing all the sweat off. I got into my street clothes and pulled my backpack out of my gym locker.

"Baltz, I'd like to see you in my office." Coach peered around the corner while I was stuffing my sweaty gym clothes into my locker for another day. We didn't have to take them home to be washed until Friday, and even then, I didn't always.

After finishing up, I knocked on the door frame of Coach Pickering's office.

"Baltz," he said, "I want you to consider training for the Winter Classic. It's a 10K."

My heart thumped. "Isn't what we do every day a 10K?" I thought six miles was about ten kilometers.

"Yes," he said, "but I can see you're not running to your potential. And I can't properly train you for it in a pack of twelve year olds."

I was confused. What did he mean?

"I want you to start training with the high school squad. Starting tomorrow."

My eyes snapped open. Wide. My jaw hung loose.

"It'll be hard. You'll be bottom of the heap, last of the pack. But you'll get the good running that you need."

Last of the pack. I nodded stupidly. So that's why he gave me today—my one moment of glory leading the way, knowing all along he was going to throw me to the wolves.

"You game for it?" he said.

"Yes, sir," I said. "I think so." The high school team!

I rode to Mr. Watson's invigorated, pedaling like a maniac, keeping, however, a sharp eye out for trucks that might run me over before my time.

High school cross-country was going to be a challenge. I'd miss Coach Pickering, but I'd be glad to leave all that praying. I'd get out of the memorizing too. Probably the high school coach was a more down-to-earth kind of guy.

By the time I arrived at Mr. Watson's, I wanted to talk about nothing but cross-country. All religious thoughts had melted away. A person like me—twelve years old, almost thirteen—in the prime of life and health, jogging along like a champion with the high school team—a person like that could worry about life and death later.

Just then there was a knock on the door. A loud, insistent knock. Moments later, Arby Jenkins burst into the kitchen and slammed himself down onto a chair like the world was going to end.

"Yo, Arb," I said.

"Hi," he said. He looked around madly, like a hunted animal. Mr. Watson slid a mug of decaf in front of him. Jenkins grabbed the handle and guzzled it like a wild man.

"What is the matter, Rutherford?" said Mr. Watson. Mr. Watson always called Arby by his real name.

"My grandma," he said, "is knitting you a sweater for Christmas!" He stared at Mr. Watson insanely. I thought briefly of calling the police.

"What color?" said Mr. Watson.

"Dark blue," he said. "Grandma said it was deep blue for a deep friendship."

I snickered. Jenkins had a problem of jumping to conclusions. Everything assumed dramatic proportions to him.

"How kind," said Mr. Watson. "It's very sweet of her."

"Are you going to marry my grandma, Mr. Watson?" Arby choked this sentence out, contorting his face. He looked as if he might cry. I sat back to enjoy the show.

"Maybe I will marry her," said Mr. Watson, "and maybe I won't." Jenkins was having hysterics, but Mr. Watson spoke with a kind firmness, and I got the idea that he had in fact been considering marriage. "But whether I do or not, you'll have to behave yourself, young man."

At this moment, I laughed out loud.

"What's the matter with you?" Arby shouted.

"I was just thinking about the time you said Mr. Watson was like a dad to me because he takes me places and lets me come over here whenever I want."

"Yeah, so what?"

"So, if he's my dad, and he marries your grandma, then you'll be my nephew."

Arby buried his face in his hands.

"Uncle Stuart," I said. "I like the sound of that." I couldn't resist going on. "And then your grandmother will be like my mom, and your mom . . . " Here I stopped for effect. "Your mom will be my sister!"

Arby stood up. He started to walk one way, then the other. Finally, he gave us one last glance and rushed out of the house. Take it from me, that kid's wound too tight.

A few sips of decaf later, I asked Mr. Watson if he was going to marry Mrs. Parsons, Arby's grandma.

"Don't you think I'm a little old for getting married?"

"No, I don't," I said. "I think it would be nice."

"Really," he said. I couldn't tell whether it was a question or a statement.

It was after eight o'clock before we sat down in the living room. The pizza delivery man had come and gone, and the last few pepperonis were happily digesting in my very full stomach. What I didn't want right now was a long tedious boring discussion about being saved.

"I think we've had a long enough day," said Mr. Watson.

What a relief. He wasn't going to corner me.

"I'll just take you on home," he said.

"I can ride," I said. "It's not that late." I didn't want Mr. Watson to see my place. He'd been there once before when he picked me up for the retreat, but that had been a while back. Maybe he'd forgotten about it.

"Okay," he said, "but take this."

He handed me a large brown envelope.

"It's something I want you to read," he said.

"Okay," I said. "Thanks for the dinner and everything."

I slid the envelope into my backpack and rode home under the stars. When I got home, no one was there. Mom was still at work, and Grandma had left a note saying she was at a church activity and wouldn't be home until ten o'clock.

I was alone for once. I settled into the big living room chair, grabbed a soda from the fridge, and pulled out Mr. Watson's envelope. Inside was a sheaf of papers, five or so, stapled together at the top. The pages were photocopied out of a book. The top of the first page said this: *Most Famous Sermon Ever Preached In America.*

Okay, I thought, reading sermons on a perfectly fine Thursday night was not my idea of having a brilliant, memorable time, but I'd humor Mr. Watson. If it was boring enough, it could only put me to sleep.

9 An Angry God

Sinners in the Hands of an Angry God was written by Jonathan Edwards in 1741 with the specific intent of scaring the daylights out of me almost three hundred years later. I could not sleep. I was afraid to move out of my chair for fear I would trip and die and be cast into hell. I was afraid to stay in my chair for fear it would collapse on me, killing me, whereupon I would drop silently and eternally into the wrath of God.

For example, his sermon said,

> *Unconverted men walk over the pit of hell on a rotten covering, and there are innumerable places in this covering so weak that they will not bear their weight, and these places are not seen.*

If that doesn't scare you, try this one:

> *The God that holds you over the pit of hell, much as one holds a spider or some loathsome insect over the fire . . . is dreadfully provoked: his wrath towards you burns like fire; he looks upon you as worthy of nothing else but to be cast into the fire.*

I tried to think about something else—anything else! I even tried to think about my dad, but the yawning abyss that *Sinners* had opened up under me breathed hot on my mind. It was only, I had learned, God's mere pleasure that I did not drop this very instant into eternal flames!

When Grandma came home, I settled down a bit. She started right in chattering about how the potluck supper had gone, and how someone had said that potlucks shouldn't be called potlucks when you have them at church because there isn't any such thing as luck.

"Ha, ha," said Grandma, "so we tried to make up a new name for potluck supper, and someone finally decided to call it a Providential Pot! Do you get it? Providence instead of luck. Isn't that nice, don't you think, Stuart?"

I must have been staring at her like she was an endangered species newly escaped from the zoo because she came over and felt my forehead.

"You don't feel hot," she said, "but Honey, you don't look so good. Do you feel okay?"

What could I say? That I could feel the lick of the flames? That I could sense myself hanging by a spider's web over the pit of hell and all she could talk about was Providential Pots?

If Mr. Watson had called that minute and asked me if I wanted to accept-the-Lord-Jesus-Christ-right-now, you better believe me when I say I would have run straight to his house, thrown myself on the floor, and begged God to have mercy on my poor wicked, wretched soul.

Instead, Mom came hollering through the door, upset because another waitress called in sick for tomorrow morning and Mom was going to have to work on her day off. There was a good deal of banging doors and shouting, throughout which I sat riveted in the chair, willing my blood pressure to even out and my pulse to return to normal.

Somehow, I don't know how, I managed to get into bed around eleven o'clock. Way too late for a school night, especially if you are going to be running with the high school cross-country team the next day, and especially if you've just been introduced to Jonathan Edwards and his famous sermon.

I did not sleep well. I had frightening dreams. Finally, I woke up scared and sweating. I prayed. Out loud.

"God," I said, "that sermon scared me to death. I am going to try to be good, really good, so that you will not throw me into hell. Please help me to be good enough. I don't want to go to hell."

I tacked on "in Jesus' name I pray, Amen," not that I knew what that meant, but it seemed to be the thing most of my friends say when they are done telling God the things they want, like good weather for the soccer game.

In the morning, the sun poured in through my open window. I was still tired, but happy that I had decided to be good so God would not be angry with me anymore. I was sure I could—now that I was going to really try—be good enough. I took a few minutes to think before I got out of bed. I thought through the situations I was likely to meet during the day. Then I made a list.

How to Be Really Good to Please God

1. Be nice to Grandma.

2. Make bed.

3. Do dishes without being asked.

4. Be polite at school to everyone.

5. Say hello to Mrs. McPherson.

6. Don't be sarcastic.

7. Let the girls go first into class.

8. Don't lie or steal.

9. Be humble about cross-country (high school team).

10. Come home on time and do homework cheerfully.

It was a good list. I got up and made my bed, making sure there were no wrinkles. I folded my pajamas and put them under my pillow, and I spent a few minutes cleaning my room. Already I was sure I was pleasing God more and more.

When I meandered out into the kitchen, I noticed that Grandma was playing the organ and singing "Shall We Gather at the River," a song she had been working on. Okay, it bothered me, but I was determined to be nice to Grandma.

"Good morning, Grandma," I said.

I poured myself some cereal, added milk and sugar, and dug in. Three bites later, I slapped my forehead. I had forgotten to pray. I bowed my head, mumbled "Thank you, God," and then continued to chow down on my Wheaties. I felt good about that prayer because it wasn't even on my list. I resolved to pray again over my lunch, and maybe even dinner.

Grandma's playing got louder and louder, and I heard an ominous noise from the other end of the trailer. Mom on the loose.

"Mother!" Mom said. "Please!"

The organ music got softer.

Mom shuffled out to the kitchen in her robe and slippers. She sat down with me at the table. She looked at me and then over at Grandma. She leaned over to me.

"We have to move, Stuart."

I nodded.

"What's that, Honey?" said Grandma.

"I was talking to Stuart, but what I said was, that he and I need to get our own place soon."

"Oh, no!" said Grandma. "You're not thinking of leaving, are you?"

"Yes, Mom, I am. Stuart's growing. I'm almost forty. We need to get back on our feet."

Grandma looked as if she'd been shot. I became very uncomfortable. I wished these grown-up decisions could be made when I wasn't there. Like maybe Mom could pick me up from school one day and say, "Guess what, Stuart; we got our own place." That way I wouldn't have to form an opinion about it; I could just show up.

"Don't take it personally, Mom," my mom said. "You have been very kind to let Stuart and me stay here. But it's been several months now, and we really need to get back on our own four feet."

"Is it the organ?" said Grandma. "I could get headphones."

"It's not the organ, Mom. It's just that we need our own place, okay?"

Well, Grandma started to get emotional. I guess she'd gotten used to us being there. She dabbed at her eyes with the back of her hand.

"Well, if it's what the Lord wants," said Grandma.

"I did not ask the Lord," said my mother. "I just decided it. I'm thirty-nine years old, and my son and I need our own place. As I said, it's been very nice of you, but it's time. I've saved a little money now and . . ."

"You have money?" said Grandma. "I thought you didn't have any. That's why I paid for Stuart's doctor's appointment."

"Now, Mom, I don't tell you everything . . ."

I could tell this was going to get worse before it got better. I did not want to be around. My ready-to-be-perfect attitude was fading fast. I already wanted to shout or hit somebody. So I got up from the table, left my dirty dishes there, grabbed my backpack, and headed out the door. I hoped God wouldn't mind that I hadn't stopped to brush my teeth.

I growled at the first person I saw, but then remembered I was on a mission to keep myself out of those everlasting flames, and I said "hello" and "how are you" to fifteen people before my first class.

In English class, I raised my hand when Mrs. McPherson asked if anyone wanted to volunteer to pray.

"Dear God," I said. "Thank you for this day. Please help us to do our best in this class. Amen."

Bingo. Chalk one up for me, Stuart W. Baltz. I could just about see those golden streets.

After English class, I ran to my locker to get my science book. I was closing my locker when some guy crashed right out of nowhere into my locker, slamming the door on my hand.

"Ouch!" I said. "You stupid fool!"

"Sorry," he said, "I'm sorry. I didn't realize . . ."

"Well, you ought to realize, you moron, that people are at their lockers!"

My hand was killing me, I thought it might be broken, and I basically wanted to murder the guy. If I got right up, I could punch his dumb lights out and still make it to science before the bell rang.

Or so I thought. As I struggled to my feet, the bell did ring, and the guy—whose name I did not know—was rushing off down the hall.

That did it.

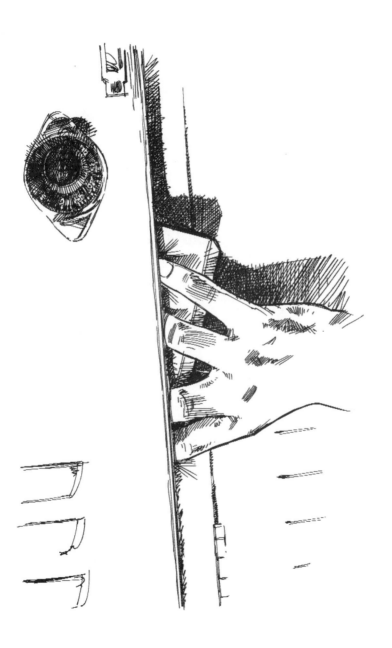

"Idiot!" I shouted. I stumbled after him shouting, "Idiot! You moron!" at the top of my lungs, willing myself to run, even though my hand was throbbing and I felt sick to my stomach.

I stopped, looked around, and realized that I was alone in the hallway, shouting words that could get me suspended if not expelled from this stupid, stinking, rotten school. And I further realized that doors on the corridor were open, and several teachers were standing in their doorways looking at me.

One of them was Mr. Hogan.

I did not cry in Mr. Thompson's office. He got the whole story out of me, called the nurse to check my hand, and then sent me home for the day.

"We cannot have that sort of behavior at GCA," he said. "But I do understand that you were sorely provoked, so we'll let it go with a one-day suspension. You can come back on Monday."

"Yes, sir." So much for being good and pleasing God. So much for cross-country practice.

10 Man-to-Man

At home Grandma would be crying or playing the electronic organ, an obnoxious instrument that I hated more and more. I told Mr. Thompson that my mom was working, and he said I could go to Mr. Watson's since he was listed on my emergency form.

I rode over there disgusted with myself. I hadn't been able to control myself even for the morning of one teeny little day of trying to be good.

Mr. Watson was waiting outside for me.

"Rough day, Stuart?" They must have called him, I thought.

"Yeah." I slid my backpack off my shoulder and threw it in a corner of his kitchen. My wrapped-up hand made me look like a boxer ready to take someone on.

"Come on," he said. I followed him to the backyard. He had bags of brown pine needles that he was arranging around the bottom of his trees. I thought it strange that something dead could make the place look better.

I helped him lay out armfuls of pine needles. Then we picked weeds out of his pansy beds, and then I mowed his lawn for him, which wasn't easy since I had only one good hand. But then, Mr. Watson has only one arm—which is another story—so I didn't like to let him mow his yard, even though he had been mowing lawns without me or his arm since 1942.

After the yard work, we went inside. He set me to vacuuming his whole house. Then we scrubbed and mopped the kitchen floor. He gave me job after job like I was his servant, but it didn't bother me. After all, I was intruding on his life on a school day, and maybe these were his regular Friday chores. And besides that, I didn't want to talk about what had happened at school. "Pass the pine needles" was more like it.

By lunch time, the whole house was as clean as I figured a house could get. Mr. Watson prayed a long prayer over bowls of steaming chili. He poured me a tall glass of milk, and when that was all done, he brought out the chocolate chip cookies.

"What happened today, son?"

"I was trying to please God."

"And this got you suspended?"

"I can't help it if some idiot barrels out of a classroom and slams into my locker and—"

"Of course you can."

"What?"

"Of course you can behave properly, even under duress."

"But I couldn't help shouting at him. The words just came out." I tried to keep my voice calm, but it got louder.

"No, they didn't just come out. You said them."

"Look, Mr. Watson," I said, "I don't need you preaching at me. I've already had a rotten day, been sent to the office, gotten suspended. I've had enough preaching, okay?"

"Stuart, I am not preaching at you. I just want you to see your own responsibility before the Lord."

"Oh, stop it, please. I'm sick and tired of all this God business. You and all the rest of them—everyone's the same, trying to make a goody-goody little Christian out of me. You even gave me that 'Angry-God' sermon to scare me spitless. I didn't sleep all night, and now I'm expelled from school, and Mom will kill me, and . . . and . . . "

"You're not expelled, just suspended. It's just one day. I'm sure we can work things out with the school."

I stood up. I was raging angry. My head was pounding, and I knew I was probably purple.

"Just stuff it, Mr. Watson. I'm out of here."

I grabbed my backpack and slammed his front door on my way out. I didn't want to go home and face Grandma's inevitable tears, so I peddled over to the public library and stomped up to a deserted corner. I sat down in a study carrel where no one could see me, put my head down on the desk, and bawled like a baby.

The problem with crying like an infant is that sooner or later you have to get on with your life and you look horrible. When I finally pulled myself together enough to think about what an awful mess I'd gotten myself into, I didn't know what to do. I'd offended everyone I knew. In the end, I pretended nothing was wrong, checked out a couple of books, and rode home like it was a normal afternoon.

Mr. Hogan was standing on my porch.

I am dog meat, I thought.

"Get in the car, Stuart," he said.

I'm toast.

Grandma was looking out the window, her fingertips held up to her mouth in a sad, frightened action.

I got in the car. What a humiliation. Mr. Hogan driving over all our potholes, skirting around little kids whose mothers let them play in the middle of the road. He got out once to move some dumb kid's Big Wheel out of the way.

Neither of us spoke. He drove straight to Cook's. I thought I was going to be ill.

"Get out, Baltz," he said.

Mr. Hogan and I walked into Cook's. Mom saw us right away and came running over.

"Is something wrong?" she said.

Mr. Hogan stuck out his hand. "William Hogan."

Mom shook his hand. "Patti Baltz," she said. She smoothed down her apron and tucked a wisp of hair behind her ear in a way that irritated me.

"Pleased to meet you," they said at the same time.

"Mrs. Baltz," said Mr. Hogan, "I would like your permission to take Stuart out for dinner tonight. He did not have a good day at school, and I thought maybe a man-to-man chat would do him some good."

"Are you the teacher who does the science experiments?" she said.

"Yes, ma'am; I try to keep things interesting."

Mom turned pink, and I think it was the "ma'am."

"Stuart likes you very much," she said.

Mr. Hogan didn't say anything, so Mom said, "Well, okay, I guess it'll be okay. Is it okay with you, Honey?"

I nodded. Yeah, sure. If a person's going to be drawn and quartered, Hogan might as well be the one doing it.

"Have a good time then, you two."

Bye, Mom, I thought. It's been nice knowing you.

"I'll have him home by nine," said Mr. Hogan.

I glanced at the clock. It was four o'clock on the nose. Five hours to go. I hoped I would live through it.

"Bye, Mom," I said.

"See you later, Sweetie," Mom said. "And good-bye, Mr. Hogan. It was nice to meet you. Stuart speaks very highly of you."

First thing we did was drive to Mr. Hogan's house. It was a large pale-peach stucco house with a landscaped lawn. It was pansy time, and there were millions of them.

"A little hobby of mine," Hogan said.

"Hi, Mom," he said as we walked through the door.

"You live with your mother?" I said. It was the first thing I had said to him. I'd always assumed that Hogan had a wife and three little babies and that he lived in a brick house with a golden retriever.

"Yes," he said. "Come meet her."

We walked around through the hallway and into the living room. An old lady with bright pink cheeks sat in a wheelchair. Mr. Hogan walked up to her and gave her a kiss and a hug.

"Mom, this is one of my students, Stuart Baltz."

"Hello," I said. "It's nice to meet you."

Mrs. Hogan nodded. "Hello," she said.

"Has the nurse been by today?" Mr. Hogan asked. He used a gentle tone of voice, not like his stern class-voice, and he knelt down on the floor so he could look at his mom straight in her sweet crinkly face.

Mrs. Hogan nodded. "She was here."

"And you've had your supper?"

She nodded again.

Mr. Hogan patted his mother's arm. "Is there anything I can get you, Mom? Stuart and I are going to be taking a little drive this evening, but I'll be back by nine-thirty to help you into bed. Will that be fine?"

She nodded. "That's fine, Sweetie."

Mr. Hogan arranged his mother's shawl and wheeled her around so she could see the television. He pulled over an end table so her water glass was handy. It had a straw so she could get at it easily. The television remote control was there, a large-print *Reader's Digest,* and a bowl of chocolate candies.

"Mom likes chocolate," he said to me.

I was strangely embarrassed by his attentive concern for his mom. I'd always thought of him as a big, strong, intimidating man, and here he was down on his knees arranging his mother's lap robe.

As we buckled up in the car, he spoke again. "Each of us has his own difficulties with the people we love the most."

We drove without speaking for a long time. I watched the digital clock on his dashboard. Minute after minute ticked by in silence. We drove out of Greenhaven altogether and made for the country.

"Where are we going?" My voice seemed out of place in the quiet car.

"You'll see."

We pulled up at the last civilized place I could see, a Burger King, and ordered Whoppers, fries, and sodas.

"No eating yet," said Mr. Hogan when I tried to dig in the bag for a French fry.

A few minutes later, he turned off on a dirt road and followed it down to a house on a small lake. The wheels crunched on the gravel driveway. An old man sat on a porch swing.

"Hey, there, William!" said the old man, waving at Mr. Hogan.

"Hi, Uncle Bob. Mind if I use your canoe?"

"Nope, you go right ahead. It's just a-sittin' there."

So we paddled out to the middle of Uncle Bob's lake and munched Whoppers and fries. It was peaceful. The lake was small and absolutely calm.

"One thing about canoes is," Mr. Hogan said, "if I rock the boat we both fall in, and if you rock the boat we both fall in."

"True," I said, smiling.

"So there's an element of trust here, yes?"

"Yes," I said.

"So if I get preachy, and you decide to dump me overboard, you realize you'll get covered with lake scum too, and we still have to drive back."

I laughed out loud at last, and my whole heart—my whole self—felt much better.

"Tell me everything, Stuart."

I figured he meant "everything," so I started at the very beginning of my life. The story tumbled out of me, paragraph after paragraph, page after page, chapter after chapter, hope after hope, fear after fear.

Mr. Hogan did not interrupt me, although he did say "go on" and other encouraging things to keep me going. I ended by telling him how I'd been so scared after reading *Sinners in the Hands of an Angry God*, and how I wanted to do good so God would be pleased with me and not send me to hell, but how it all fell apart around me, and how horrible I felt when I knew He knew how bad I was, and how miserable I felt when I shouted at Mr. Watson.

"I want to please God, Mr. Hogan, really I do."

"And why is that, do you think?"

"Because I am afraid of hell. I do not want to go to hell."

"Why not?"

"Well, it's eternal, burning flames, and it's the everlasting anger of God."

"And you think you can appease the anger of God by making your bed and saying hello to Mrs. McPherson?"

I suddenly saw how silly my list was. Make Bed. Be Nice. Come Home on Time. Do Homework.

"I guess not," I said. "What *can* I do then?"

"Absolutely nothing whatsoever."

"Well, there must be something," I said. "I've got to get out of hell somehow."

"Nope," he said, "there's not a thing you can do to get yourself out of hell. Not if you work at it for the rest of your life."

"Why not?"

"Because the Bible says your good works are as filthy rags. Frankly, Stuart, you're a sinner. Your whole life is stained with sin—hey, don't rock the boat; we'll fall in."

I steadied myself. I had heard this before somewhere. Maybe back at camp? Or from Mr. Watson? Or school?

"Wait," I said. "I know this verse. Something about wages for sin."

"Yes, the wages of sin is death. Anyone who sins deserves eternal damnation in hell. That's God's Word on the matter. Nothing we try to do about it will change it. We cannot scrape our sins off ourselves. They're indelible. They don't come off. It takes a more powerful solvent than being good."

I sat slumped in the canoe. I was beaten. I was down. And stuck in the middle of the lake with Mr. Hogan. Hogan, who in a million trillion years did not have to take the time to talk with me like this.

"All the Bible stuff is true?" I said.

"Every word of it."

"Okay," I said, "tell me from the beginning." I said this because I knew Mr. Hogan was right when he said my sins were stuck to me and that nothing I could do would get them off. I couldn't work them off or wish them away. I couldn't pretend they weren't there. I was covered up with slimy lake-scum sins, clinging to me, drawing me down into the wrath of God.

I had heard it before, but I had not really listened with my whole self. That Jesus was God, that He came to earth to take all our sins onto Himself. To pay for them with His own blood. I remembered the song:

What can wash away my sin?

"So when Jesus Christ died on the cross, He was carrying all the guilt of all the sins of all mankind, Stuart. And God judged that sin, right there at Calvary. He poured out His wrath against sin on Jesus, His only Son."

Nothing but the blood of Jesus.

Mr. Hogan fell silent for a while and paddled us around to another part of the lake. It was getting dark now. Keep talking, Mr. Hogan, I thought. It was beginning to break through my thick head. It was all beginning to make sense.

What can make me whole again? Nothing but the blood of Jesus.

"Jesus died for me," I said. "So God won't have to punish me in hell."

"Stuart, if you will trust Christ to save you, He will save you. You will be a child of God, an heir of heaven. You will not need to fear hell anymore. You will become a child of God. The Bible says all who come to Christ belong to Him and can never be cast out of His hand. You'll be safe."

"Will I be good?"

"You will be safe from hell forever. And yes, your desires will change from wanting to please yourself to wanting to please God."

"Will I be able to please God then?"

"Nothing we do has any merit with God, Stuart. It's only through Christ and His work on the cross that we are accepted by God."

Our conversation trailed off. I thought about the burden of my many sins and how I couldn't be good. I knew full well God wasn't pleased with me and that I couldn't do any better than I had done already, that on my own I couldn't be good for even part of one day. And now I could see that even if I did do better, it wouldn't scrape off all the old sins that clung to me like chains, weighing me down into hell.

Would you be free from the burden of sin?

I needed a Savior.

There's wonderful power in the blood.

And there was a Savior. And He died for me. But there was something else, it seemed. I dredged my memory.

"Jesus came back to life, Mr. Hogan?"

"Yes, Stuart. When Christ died, He took the penalty—that is, He took the whole wrath of God for all our sins. But when He rose again three days later, it proved that He had power over death. That's why we can be sure that He is powerful enough to raise those of us who believe on Him. He will take us out of death and into heaven."

That made sense. If Jesus had stayed dead, then how could He be powerful enough to save me from hell?

"Mr. Hogan," I said, "I need a Savior. I want to trust Jesus Christ to save me."

There is a fountain filled with blood drawn from Immanuel's veins.

Mr. Hogan and I—we prayed in that little canoe in the middle of the lake under a darkening, starry sky. I prayed that God would save me, that the blood of Jesus Christ, God's Son, would cleanse me from all my sins. I also asked God to help me please because I had been a rotten person at home and at school and being a Christian was not going to be easy for me.

Mr. Hogan prayed long and fervently that I would grow up to be a servant of the Lord. This made me feel loved and strong and hopeful. He thanked God for seeing us two miserable sinners, William Hogan and Stuart Baltz, and having mercy on our poor souls. He prayed for a long time, but for once it didn't bother me. I felt a deep peace inside me, and I knew I was safe.

And sinners plunged beneath that flood lose all their guilty stains.

11 My Own Words

"I don't know how to be a Christian," I said to Mr. Hogan as we drove down the highway back to town. "What if I get back to Greenhaven, away from all this, and I find out that it's just too hard."

"Let me teach you a couple of words, Stuart," he said. "The first one is *justification.* Justification is God's act of saving your miserable soul. That's what happened when God gave you the faith to believe the gospel, out there on the lake.

"The other word is *sanctification.* Sanctification is the process of growing into holiness. It takes time, sanctification does. You make progress and you slip back, but your eyes remain fixed on Christ and you continue to become like Him."

"Thank you, Mr. Hogan," I said. We'd negotiated the potholes and pulled up to my house at ten minutes till nine. "And pray for me, will you, please? When I tell my grandma I'm a Christian, she's going to fall apart in little chunks all over the ground. Mom will fall apart too, but I don't think she'll be happy."

"She'll need time to see you *be* a Christian," he said. "But don't worry—God will help you."

And he was gone.

Mom and Grandma were reading when I walked in.

"Hi, Honey," they both said at once.

"Hi," I said. Then, never having been a person who put things off, I got right to it.

"You'll be glad to know that I've been saved," I said. "I've trusted Christ to forgive my sins and take me to heaven when I die. It may take me a while to get the hang of Christianity, but it's a done deal—I'm saved—so don't try to talk me out of it."

I kissed both of them and walked into my room. Then I stuck my head out one last time.

"And no, Mr. Hogan didn't tell me to say any of that. Those were my own words."

I went to bed and slept like a log.

12 Different

I sat on the bench feeling skinny and babyish in my running clothes while the varsity track team milled around me, oblivious to my fright, and even my existence. I am not normally a squeamish individual, but these guys were gigantic. I felt like one of the people in the town overridden with steroid-enhanced frogs, waiting to be squashed. Why was I here, anyway? Some dumb idea Coach Pickering had about me running the Winter Classic with the varsity team. As if I'd make it in a group of guys whose forearms were thicker than my thighs.

The whole weekend had been surreal. My first thought upon waking up Saturday was that I felt something was different about today. Then I remembered—I had become a Christian! I bounded out of bed, reached for my Bible like I'd been reading it every morning of my life, and read the first three chapters of Genesis. Why not start at the beginning?

After that, I'd ridden over to Mr. Watson's house, apologized for my abominable behavior of the day before, and blurted out the news of my being saved. Then I'd ridden past Arby and Ray who were walking down the street, kicking a rock in front of them.

"Hey, you guys, I got saved last night!"

"Really? No, kidding? What?" These and other strange comments came from Jenkins, who didn't quite know what to say. I got through all of Saturday and Sunday feeling kind of light, and sort of different. Like everyone was looking at

me. Like I was a Martian or Venusian, and not just a Christian like almost everyone else in my life.

Monday at lunch time, Arby and Ray ate with me and asked me what had happened. I told them all about it. They were nicer to me than usual, and in fact, the whole day seemed to be going unusually well.

Until now.

I was squashed in the locker room between two monster-sized high schoolers who did not seem to notice that there was not room for all three of us on the bench, but I couldn't move because I was squished. I began to wonder if Coach Pickering had really meant what he'd said about me reporting to the varsity team. What if the varsity coach hadn't heard about me? What if the coach asked me what I was doing there?

"Yo, Baltz, come here."

I looked up. Dell Jenkins. What a relief. I eased myself out from between the two trolls.

"Sit over here," Dell said. "Those guys are a couple of Neanderthals."

I laughed.

"Coach told us you were coming." Dell paused. "You scared?"

"Out of my mind," I said. "But it's okay. I got saved last Friday night."

"Cool," said Dell. "Does Arby know? He's been praying for you."

"Yeah, I told him."

It seemed strange to be having a man-to-man talk about my getting saved with Arby's big brother who was, after all, fifteen years old and in the tenth grade. My experience had been that tenth graders treated seventh graders like people who had bubonic plague.

"What's your coach like?" I asked.

"It's Thompson."

"Mr. Thompson?"

"The same."

"I'll die," I said. "Mr. Thompson hates me. I'm in his office all the time. He's going to kick me out of school if I flub one more time."

"So don't flub," he said.

Good point, I thought. I wouldn't flub. I'd do my best and trust God to help me. Now that I was a Christian, everything would be just fine. My life would ease into a refined and stable level.

Five miles later, I was not feeling so confident. The fact was, high school boys run faster than junior high boys. I was reaching deep inside myself for every step, willing myself to go on, stretching with every stride not to be too far behind the last guy. And failing. I was the tail end. Bottom of the barrel. End of the line. The last banana.

By the time we got back to school, I was spent, beat up, and coughing.

"Good job, Baltz," Dell said.

"Well done, Stuart," Mr. Thompson said.

I think I'm going to die, I thought.

Good thing I got saved.

13 Scientific Deductions

One thing started to bug me about the kids at school after I became a Christian. I began to have niggling thoughts that a whole lot of them didn't know anything about Christianity, like Steven Adams, for example.

Or, I would overhear people talking about how they couldn't stand someone.

"Have you seen Tiffy?" one of the girls would say.

"Yeah," another would say, "she thinks she's such a hoity-toity, and her mom lets her wear full makeup and double-pierced ears!"

Then these same girls would pray in class, sing specials in chapel, or even give testimonies at lunch time Bible studies. I didn't get it, so I asked Mr. Hogan.

"Is this what you mean by hypocrisy?" I said.

"Bring it up in class," he said. "I'll make it easy for you, and then we can have a class discussion. I think it will be extremely interesting."

So that's what happened. In science class the next day—I'd been saved about a week—Mr. Hogan sat on the edge of his desk and surveyed the room, giving me a meaningful glance, which I knew was a cue.

"Do you think," he said, "that a person's Christianity could be deduced scientifically?"

Huh? This wasn't the lead-in I'd expected. I didn't say anything. What about hypocrisy? No one else did either. I felt like I was letting Mr. Hogan down.

"Let me ask that another way," he said. "How can I know a person is a Christian, using the scientific method?"

Groans filled the air. We'd been tested and re-tested on the scientific method so many times we thought we'd never get over it. And then, at last, when everyone in the class finally got all five points correct on the quiz, Mr. Hogan had let it go. Until now. I knew the scientific method like the back of my hand. It goes like this:

1. Look. Make observations.

2. Write. Record the changes.

3. Compile. Accumulate the information.

4. Think. Analyze the findings.

5. Predict. Formulate a hypothesis.

Scientists use this method to figure things out, and Mr. Hogan had taught us that it is generally accepted that this method must be applied to all scientific efforts.

Mr. Hogan had also taught us that the scientific method is what keeps the theory of evolution from being a fact.

"Remember, class," he'd said, "the Darwinian theory of evolution by natural selection cannot be observed or recorded. It is never seen in the world today, so we can't accumulate information about it. There aren't any."

"So why do people believe in evolution?" someone asked.

"What's the alternative?" he said.

"That God created the world."

"Right."

He left it there, and it had sure given me something to chew on since back then I was a Cro-Magnon believer and didn't give the time of day to people who really thought God created the world out of nothing at all in less than a week. It had taken me a whole week to make my vinegar and baking soda volcano last year.

However, now—now that I was a Christian—it made sense. If God could forgive my sins because of Christ and give me eternal life, obviously He had given me life as a human being in the first place.

In any case, today Mr. Hogan wanted to know if we could apply the scientific method to figuring out if someone was a Christian.

"Well?" His voice boomed over our ignorant silence.

Sometimes I felt smart to be in the seventh grade, and other times I felt really stupid. Like now.

"No, sir." A voice floated up from the back of the room.

"Why not?"

"Because Christians don't always act like Christians, so your observation might be wrong."

"Yeah," I said, seeing my opening. "Like sometimes I overhear people around this school who are supposed to be Christians, but they're ridiculing other people or shunning them, or whatever, and then they go and pray in English class like a bunch of hoity-toities."

I took a deep breath and realized my sentence was too long. Nobody said anything, and I felt foolish.

"True," said Mr. Hogan.

"Also," someone else said, "you can't record information. You can't go around writing people's behavior down and analyzing it."

"You could," I said. "Like Grammar Infractions."

"Grammar Infractions has been abolished," a boy said, "as if you didn't remember."

"I remember, I remember," I said.

We decided at last that it should be possible to tell if a person is a Christian by the way he acts.

"What about nonbelievers who act like Christians?" Mr. Hogan's new question sat in the air. "This might include people who have pleasant personalities and practical integrity in their lives; or perhaps people of other religions who are strict in their behaviors."

Mr. Hogan didn't mind if we raised our hands or not during general discussions, so the opinions began to fly.

"I know people like that. Lots of them."

"My grandma always tells us to *Stop It* when we try to witness to her, but she's very nice otherwise."

"Some people think they're Christians, and they're not."

"My dad says he's a Christian, but you can't tell by watching him."

"Hmm," said Mr. Hogan. "Then is it possible that people in this room think they're Christians and act like Christians, but aren't really Christians?"

Everyone looked around at one another. It reminded me of a sermon I'd heard Pastor Snyder preach once about Jesus telling His disciples one of them was going to give Him away to the bad guys. They all looked around at each other too, not knowing who it was.

"Yes," said a girl. "Because I thought I was a Christian for several years before I was saved."

"That's interesting, Katy," said Mr. Hogan. "Would you like to tell us about it?"

"Well, okay," Katy said. She seemed kind of nervous, but I was rooting for her. So many kids at this Christian school seemed to not want to talk about Christian stuff. But Katy was our class president, so it encouraged me that she was willing to be an upfront Christian.

"When I was four years old, I said a prayer in Sunday school like: 'Dear Jesus, please come into my heart.' But the summer after fifth grade, I went to Bible camp. While I was there, I really listened to the preacher giving the plan of salvation. I understood the gospel—that Jesus died to save me, that His blood washes away the sins of those who accept Him, and that if I trusted Him I would go to heaven. I realized that I needed to turn from my sin to the Savior."

"So the prayer you prayed when you were four years old didn't count?" Mr. Hogan said.

"I didn't have any understanding," Katy said. "I guess I just wanted to please my Sunday school teacher. I had no idea what I was doing."

"But during all that time you acted like a Christian?"

"Of course," Katy said. "I was just a kid. What could I do—rob a bank?"

Everyone laughed, even Mr. Hogan, but lots of kids seemed thoughtful after Katy's story. Pretty soon the bell rang.

"So, lots to think about, guys," Mr. Hogan said. "Maybe tomorrow we'll do some more scientific method."

I stayed after class to talk to Mr. Hogan. And to report that my first week of Christianity was buzzing along fine.

"My mom's happy that I'm happy. My grandma's happy. I sat through church without falling asleep. I haven't lost my temper."

"That's great, Stuart," he said. "But remember, Christianity is not about being perfect. It's about Christ's perfection being imputed to you."

I didn't know the word—but I didn't ask either. Cross-country was next, and I knew I'd better get there on time. I figured I could never really keep up with the varsity guys, but I was at least determined to start with them.

The afternoon was overcast. I pulled on my running shorts and snatched a quick look at myself in the locker room mirror before trotting outside. I thought I cut a fairly dashing figure for a kid completely out of his league. Today, however, I was hanging onto a verse I'd learned in Bible class.

"I can do all things through Christ which strengtheneth me," Mr. Kirby had quoted. "Class, this means that anything we ought to do, we can do as Christians—through the power of the Holy Spirit working through us."

I had sat in Bible class eating this up. Bible class had begun to make sense, now that I'd accepted the gospel. I was storing away Bible verses in my mind right and left. Such as the one in Romans about all things working together for good to those who love God. I was clutching to that verse like a life preserver. It meant that all the horrible things—my dad leaving me, living in the trailer park—that were sewn into my life were part of God's plan for me and would work out someday.

But here was a new verse, about God strengthening His people. I held onto it as I bounded through the first of our six kilometers. I felt like a combination of the apostle Paul and the Little Engine that Could: "I think I can, I think I can . . . I can do all things, I can do all things."

Running with the Big Boys wasn't the skip-to-my-Lou that junior high cross-country had been. I had to crank out every horsepower I had.

Yesterday, I had crashed during the wind sprints when I was trying to prove to Coach Thompson that I belonged on the varsity team. I literally tried to make a long stride to beat one guy, for crying out loud, but when I was lunging for glory, I tripped and fell forward onto my knees, skinning them up. Quite a nasty fall—with dirt and little rocks ground into my knees.

"Slow down, Baltz," Coach Thompson had said. "Keep your own level."

"Huh?"

"Try your best, but remember, you're not these guys."

I was dying to be one of the guys. To beat one of the guys. It became my focus. I forgot about that other verse I'd learned, about thinking of myself in higher terms than I deserved. If I could just come in ahead of one—just one!—of my teammates on one run, I would be satisfied.

I broke a sweat early and hoped I wouldn't actually dehydrate from fluid loss as I drip dripped through kilometers number two and three. I was hurting, and it was becoming difficult to get enough oxygen with each breath.

Got to beat him, Got to beat him cadenced through my head with every step. By the end of the fifth kilometer, I realized I was in sight of my goal. If I ignored Coach Thompson's advice on working within my own level, if I never-minded his rule about advancing from skill strength to skill strength, if, in short, I forced myself just a shekel harder, I could finish this race ahead of one of the ninth graders who appeared to be somewhat wheezy. I pushed.

I noticed the warning signals—the shortness of breath, the serious ache in the legs, the crushing weight of my chest—as I gasped for each molecule of oxygen. I should have listened to those signals and backed off. Left the heroics for another day. But all I could see was the unclouded glory of finishing next-to-last. Rounding the corner onto the school property, I eased ahead of the freshman with one long fluid stride and thought, "Yes, I can do all things through Christ who . . . "

And fell.

14 Healing Time

I do not remember the events leading up to the moment when I opened my eyes, noticed the milling professionals in teal-green hospital scrubs, and felt the squeeze of Mom's hand on mine. Mr. Hogan stood beside her with a stern expression etched onto the granite of his face.

"Baby, are you okay?" I was alive enough to wish she hadn't called me Baby in front of Mr. Hogan.

I nodded.

"What happened, Stuart?" Mr. Hogan asked.

"I fell."

"Yes, I know. But what happened?" His voice had a calm, tell-me-everything note.

"I thought I could do all things through Christ who strengtheneth me."

Mr. Hogan smiled. Mom looked over at him with question marks in her eyes.

"Is this something Stuart was taught at school, Mr. Hogan?"

"Please," he said, "call me William."

"Is it, Stuart?"

I sighed. "I don't know."

"What we have here," Mr. Hogan said, "is a classic case of applying a Scripture unscripturally. Give me the straight low-down, Mr. Baltz."

There are some adults who can be schmoozed. Mr. Hogan was not one of them.

"I wanted to beat one kid. I didn't want to be the last one home."

Mom laughed. "That's just what you said it must have been, Mr. Hogan."

"William," he said.

"William."

I hobbled around on crutches for three weeks while my torn ligament healed. It was not a fun time, but I got a lot of sympathy from the girls at school—even Grace—and that almost made my injury worthwhile. It did not, however, lessen the hot shame I felt every time I recalled flinging myself bodily in front of a ninth grader to ward off a last place finish. I should have known better than to think a scriptural promise was intended to keep me from being the caboose.

Of course I couldn't go to cross-country practice now. But that gave me an excuse to go by Mr. Hogan's room after school. He was usually busy grading papers, but he would take the time to talk to me about life or being a Christian, and, of course, being Hogan, he always shot straight.

"You'll learn, Stuart," Mr. Hogan said during one of these after-school talks. "No one expects you to know and understand the entire Bible and all its meanings as soon as you became a Christian. That's why you've got a lifetime of learning ahead of you. Take this as a gentle lesson."

"Gentle?"

"Oh, yes. This was a gentle lesson. You hurt no one but yourself. The school insurance picked up the hospital tab. And you're on the way to a full recovery. This is what I call an encapsulated learning event. Be glad."

"You're saying it could have been worse?"

"Stuart," Mr. Hogan said. He put down his pen and assumed that faraway look he reserved for telling us huge ideas and hoping they crammed themselves into our pea-sized junior high brains. "Supposing, just supposing, that you did not learn the lesson of staying within the bounds of God's will for your life—"

He paused, and I thought this through carefully. Trying to follow him.

"And just suppose that later in your life, God uses you in some type of Christian service, such as, say, missionary work."

Me? This thought jarred me like lightning.

"And just suppose with me that you have a family and a mission relying on you for leadership."

Me?

"It would be important in that case, would it not, for you to know to stay within the bounds of the will of God."

"Yes, sir."

"Why?"

"Because it would be so important. People would be depending on me."

"Right."

I wasn't sure how this related to running. Maybe it did, and maybe it didn't. It didn't matter. I was skewered by the thought that God might use me—Stuart Baltz, father-abandoned, trailer-parked, just-got-saved, me—in His service. It made me want to jump up and run around.

Unfortunately, a person can't run too well on crutches. And I was saddled with these for several weeks. Lumbering home without my bike took longer, of course. Long enough to let my emotions swing from the big Up of thinking God might use me to the Down of realizing what I'd lost through my stupid attempt at outrunning a high schooler. The Winter Classic was nixed. My Wheaties box was nowhere in sight. And that left my longed-for unexpected phone call from my dad way off in the landfill of Maybe Someday.

The thought of all the things I had blown over a classic case of Me-first-itis hurt more than the "Yo, Crutch" and "Hey, Hop-a-long" that neighbor kids shouted at me all the way home.

15 Thanksgiving

And then Thanksgiving came out of nowhere and slapped me in the face. This holiday was an annual frenzied ritual of my whole family descending on Great-Aunt Enid. Every year we'd invade this old lady's house and pretend we were having the time of our lives watching football games and eating turkey sandwich after turkey sandwich until the world was no longer a happy place to live.

Great-Aunt Enid was my grandmother's sister. She was eighteen years old when my grandma was born, a circumstance difficult for me to comprehend. She was seventy-nine years old, and the tradition of having Thanksgiving dinner at her house went back to 1949. That was the year her husband died of wounds suffered during World War II. It took him five years to die of these wounds, but Aunt Enid was still talking about it. Basically she was angry with the government for not giving Great-Uncle Herman the Medal of Honor for risking his life to save his comrades in a heroic effort that wounded him fatally, though it took five years to actually kill him.

"He should've got that medal, believe you me," Great-Aunt Enid said. "But he was half-German, so it didn't matter. He could've single-handedly pulverized the Reichstag, and no one would have noticed."

Every year she said this, and every year people went along with her and said, "That's right, Enid; what's a Purple Heart when he should have had the Medal of Honor?"

"Hear, hear," someone would say, "to Herman!" And someone would raise his water glass. Everyone would clink glasses, hoping this would somehow make it all better for old Aunt Enid.

So I dreaded Thanksgiving because we all had to tramp over there and stay in Aunt Enid's great big house—driving four hours to get there and then sleeping on air mattresses among contingents and battalions of second and third cousins I never saw other than once a year for the annual commemoration of Uncle Herman's decease.

In spite of my best hopes, Thanksgiving arrived.

I wiped Aunt Enid's sloppy kiss off my lips as soon as I got past her. If there's one thing worse than being kissed by an old aunt, it's to be kissed on the lips by one. I hobbled back to the usual bedroom and threw my suitcase on the floor.

The table was piled high with the usual Thanksgiving feast by the time everyone had arrived. I sat between my mom and her cousin Veleen, an enormous woman who wore tight clothes and orange lipstick. I had hated her for years— not just because she weighed four hundred pounds and smacked her lips when she ate. She was also rude.

Every year she'd bring up something to me about my dad, as if I wanted to talk about him with a woman who horrified me and whom I only saw once a year. Last year, right when I was getting serious about my turkey, she asked me if my dad had started sending child support yet. I had stared at her for one monstrous second like she was an escaped maniac before returning to my food, less tasty after looking at her. I stared at her now and wondered how I was supposed to be a good testimony before a woman who appalled me. Sitting by her was a bad dream come true.

This year it turned into a nightmare.

We were all seated. Everyone's plate was heaped with food, and everyone was looking at Great-Aunt Enid, whose first bite signified the green light for chowing down. Before she could take a forkful of sweet potatoes with marshmallows, my grandma's voice erupted over the seventeen other voices.

"May we thank God for the food, please?"

Forks clattered noisily onto plates. No one said anything, and so Grandma just prayed. I was embarrassed of her and proud of her at the same time. I wished I had thought of it.

I plunged into my mashed potatoes and gravy. The football game murmured in the background. No one had bothered to turn it off. For a moment I had the mistaken idea that this dinner was going to be a cheerful family function. Then the horror began.

"Oh, Patti," said Cousin Veleen, "I'm so sorry about Philip."

Philip, meaning my dad. I couldn't believe Veleen would bring him up, Thanksgiving after Thanksgiving. Did she have no feelings whatsoever?

"Please, Veleen," Mom said. "All that is over and done with."

"Oh," said Veleen, "I thought you would have taken it more to heart."

"Veleen, please," Mom said, her voice tensing with clipped-off words. "It's been ten years. I've gone on. I have a new life now." Mom smiled at Veleen, and I felt this was extremely kind of her.

"Oh, dear," said Veleen. "You haven't heard."

Mom put her fork down slowly. She wiped her mouth with her napkin and turned to face Veleen.

So, I wanted to scream, *how IS the Medal of Honor campaign going? Doesn't anyone want to talk about Great-Uncle Herman?*

"What is it, Veleen?" Mom said. Her face was white.

"You really haven't heard?" Veleen asked in a self-conscious way that I hated.

"Veleen, you fool." That was Great-Aunt Enid.

"Veleen," said my mother. "What about Philip?"

"He's dead," Veleen said in a flat voice. "Two months ago. Sorry. I thought you knew."

I grabbed for my mother's hand. She clenched hard.

"It was an accident," Veleen said, pushing a hunk of bread into her fat face. "His brakes failed, and he ran into a semi. I read it in the Chicago paper. Sorry."

"Let's go, Stuart." Mom's voice was quiet. I pushed my chair back and left all my shattered dreams at that table. The air was filled with voices calling Veleen names and asking us please not to go. I don't know how we got to the car, but when we got there, Grandma was with us.

"I'll drive," Grandma said.

"Thanks, Mom," Mom said.

Mom cried all the way home. I sat in the back seat with my face shoved into a pillow and tears running out of my eyes like a river of hope over a waterfall.

I took my Wheaties collection down that night and threw it away. What did it matter if I became famous and got my face on the Wheaties box now? You can't make a dead person love you.

16 Starting Over

I stumbled through the weeks following Thanksgiving. I felt disconnected from myself, torn away from my own hopes and dreams. I couldn't run. My leg was on the mend, but I was benched for the year. I couldn't sit by the phone waiting for my dad to call. I couldn't rage against Mrs. McPherson. I could do nothing but go through endless day after endless day, waiting for the edges of my wounded heart to come together.

Of course, I spilled my guts about my dad to Mr. Watson. I'd been to visit him the Friday after Thanksgiving, the very next day. He piled up a plate of turkey sandwiches.

"Eat," he'd said. "And talk. There's something on your mind."

I told him every horrible detail.

"I lost something once," he said.

I looked at his empty sleeve and nodded.

"Maybe it was sort of the same," he said. "I don't know."

His arm, my dad. How the same?

"When my arm was wounded, I still had it, but it was not healthy for me. Wasn't doing me any good. Wouldn't be doing me any good. They had to take it off."

It's not quite the same, I thought. No way. A person could have reformed—come back—if he'd lived. An arm, if it's gone, it's gone.

"Oh," I said, still thinking.

"Maybe it's not the same," he said.

"That's okay."

"There is a verse for you," he said. "Just a minute, let me get it." He thumbed through his old beat-up Bible, the one that looked like it might be old enough to have been with him on his World War II ship. "Here it is. 'Trust in the Lord and do good; so shalt thou dwell in the land, and verily thou shalt be fed.' "

Okay, I thought. What's the point?

"One day at a time, Stuart," Mr. Watson said. "Just trust in the Lord each day. This is a real loss for you, and it won't be instantly healed. But God will take you through the sorrow to the other side."

"The other side?"

"Of loss. It's peace."

When I talked to Mr. Hogan, he didn't give me any speeches or verses or anything. He just sat there staring out the window.

"Sorry, Baltz," he said. "I'm so sorry."

That was all he said.

And, of course, November finally eased into December, and Christmas closed in upon us. I felt the need for Mom and me to move out of Grandma's trailer more than ever before.

I wanted Mom to be able to deck her own halls. I wanted to start over in a new place. Visions of a stucco house like Mr. Hogan's played havoc with my imagination. Mom had said she'd been saving money. Who knew what the possibilities were?

I made up a song about the trailer park:

Home, home in the dumps,

Where the potholes cover the ground.

Where everything is heard

'Cuz the walls are so thin,

And the skies can be seen

Through the roof.

Okay, I'll admit it. It wasn't artistic, it didn't rhyme, and wasn't even true, but it made me feel better about living there.

Then one day it happened.

Mom picked me up at school, tossed my bike onto the roof-rack of the car, and said, "Get in."

"Where are we going?"

"You'll see."

We drove past the trailer park, past the apartment complexes, past the cemetery, past the city limits. Into a dirt driveway. She turned the car off in front of a small blue frame house on half an acre of bare ground. It was the smallest house I'd ever seen. I walked around it in a daze. The back of the house seemed to be falling off. Three corners of the house sat on cement blocks. The fourth corner sat on a rotting stump.

"Well, what do you think?" Mom made a gesture like ta-da-look-what-I-found, and walked to the front door, key in hand.

"Are we living here?" I asked, stunned.

"You and me."

"Right now?"

"Right now. I moved while you were at school. I was afraid it wouldn't work out, so I didn't tell you until I was sure."

I walked through the front door in a daze of unbelief. A scraggly Christmas tree sat plumb in the middle of the smallest living room I had ever seen. The tree took up what little space there was. I eased my way around the tree. Then I wandered through the rest of the little rooms—it didn't take long—and stood in my room. There was my bed on the floor, and my clothes hung on a pole in the corner. The room was smaller than my room at Grandma's.

"Out of that trailer at last," Mom said, smiling, and she gave me a hug.

The house, it turned out, had belonged to Mr. Faladini's mother. She had died last summer, and Mr. Faladini and his sister had finally cleared the place out. He'd asked my mom if she'd like to rent it.

"I told him, 'Look, Mr. Faladini, you're my boss; you know how much money I make.' But he gave me a good deal on it, so here we are."

She looked at me, her eyes triumphant. "What do you think, Stuart?"

My emotions crowded in upon each other. I had hoped for a big wonderful stucco house with a lawn to mow, an extra room for a Ping-Pong table, and an Irish setter.

"I think," I said slowly, "I think it's great. It's falling apart, but it's better than the trailer park."

Somehow, though, I wasn't sure.

And then she dropped the bomb.

"Well, good. We'll settle in. You'll finish out the week at GCA, and then on Monday, I'll take you over to Hamilton Junior High."

17 Too Much

A council of war met on the South Lawn at lunch. It was Tuesday, and I had only three days after today at Greenhaven. Now that I was a Christian, I *wanted* to attend GCA. The thought of Hamilton Junior High had pulverized me. Had made me break my silence during prayer request time.

It was during World History. Miss Ward, our teacher, had just collected our homework assignments and called roll.

"Are there any prayer requests?"

My hand shot up. My voice shook.

"This is my last week of school."

It was all I could say. I couldn't find voice to say, Pray that I'll be able to stay here through some miraculous intervention of God, or pray that I'll be a good witness for Christ at Hamilton. Just the bald facts.

She didn't wait for any other requests, but bowed her head right then and began to pray.

"Dear Father in Heaven," she prayed, "Stuart has a need. This is his last week of school. We do not know how You will order this situation, but we beg you to hear us in Jesus' name, that Your holy will be done in Stuart's life."

I appreciated that prayer immensely. The guys also decided to hold council to figure out a solution.

"You've *got* to stay at GCA," Arby said. "You just got saved. God knows this and will let you stay."

"It's the money," I said. "Mom paid tuition because she didn't have to pay rent. Now she is renting a house, so there's no money."

"We will raise the money."

My heart soared. That was Ray Sanchez talking, and when Ray Sanchez talked, well, things were bound to happen. He got up and marched away in the direction of the school office. While he was gone, we guys held a belching contest. I'm not sure, but I think belching contests are an American-guy milestone, sort of like when girls get to wear lip-gloss.

A few minutes later, Sanchez wandered back, hands shoved in pockets, head down.

"Bad news, Baltzman," he said. "I found out some really bad news."

This was not the greeting I had wanted. He was supposed to say, "Yo, dudes, the plan has been formulated."

"Did you know," he said, "that it costs two hundred and forty-five dollars a month for a kid to go to Greenhaven Christian Academy?"

"Two hundred and forty-five dollars?"

"Every month."

I shuddered. This wasn't piggy-bank money, for sure.

"Check it out." Ray unfolded a piece of paper he'd scrounged out of his pocket. "I was just over in the business office digging for this information."

The guys crowded around him while he pointed to various numbers that indicated different fees for things like books, registration, insurance. All things you had to pay for, in addition to the two forty-five a month tuition. I looked up at the empty blue sky and wondered why it didn't fill up with massive nimbus clouds like we'd been learning about in science. The kind that were full of minuscule particles of dust that made huge clouds begin to rain their hearts out.

"So," he said, "with ten months of tuition, plus a hundred for registration, one twenty-five for books—" I tuned him out and thought how ironic it was.

All year long I'd wanted to get out of here. But then, I'd become a Christian. I thought this would have made things in my life improve. But no, everything seemed to be collapsing beneath me like that flimsy cover over hell Jonathan Edwards had written about.

That was one comfort, at least. There was no hell beneath my feet anymore. But what *was* underneath? I wondered. When the floor of life collapsed under a Christian, what was there?

". . . for a grand total of three thousand, one hundred fifty-two dollars per year."

"Whoa."

"Yikes."

"No wonder my mom works."

These and other gasps of enlightened minds fluttered around me. Obviously, the war council would disperse.

"However," said Sanchez, "we are not going to give up."

"We're not?" I said, yanked back into the moment.

"No. I have ideas."

"Such as?"

"Work, Baltz. We'll all work—pool our cash, start a fund."

It was a hopeless case. All those times I'd heard chapel speakers talk about the sacrifices parents made to send their kids to Christian schools suddenly made sense to me. Me, a kid who loaded the dishwasher for twenty-five cents. Me, the kid who picked weeds for cookies and decaffeinated coffee. A whole new sense of the adult world broke over me like too-heavy clouds.

Ray talked on, me vaguely hearing him, nodding at the appropriate places, giving opinions. Not believing him.

I walked to my next class in a daze. I looked at each person individually, trying to imprint his face on my memory. Even the people I had never spoken with. I sighed right out loud in class.

On the way to science class, I caught up with Grace and walked a couple of paces behind her, like she was the Queen of England and I was her willing and obedient consort. Pretending that maybe later, when I was in high school, I could find a way to come back and remind her I existed.

18 Underneath?

"Shades on."

Mr. Hogan rose out of his seat and towered before us.

I snapped my sunglasses open and crammed them onto my face. It didn't matter that they were pink, or that I had to dig them out of a box labeled "Miscellaneous Junk" that morning. It didn't even matter—at this moment—that it was now Wednesday and I was less than three days from out of here.

"Attention."

I stood by my desk and grabbed my science stuff, packing it under my arm.

"About-face."

I executed a smart one-eighty and stood facing the back of the room. The command "forward march" did not faze me. I had turned, in those few instants, into a Hogan-controlled robot. This is what happens when you love someone or you are really afraid of them. You do what they say without asking why. With Hogan it was love and fear combined, and I wasn't ashamed to admit to either feeling. Especially when I was feeling sentimental about everything at this place I used to abhor.

We hup-two-three'd it out the door, past the other classrooms, and onto the football field. Each of us carried a sketch-pad, a supply of colored pencils, and a lawn chair. We parked ourselves on the field and looked up into the sky. Even the sky had cooperated with Mr. Hogan's cloud-drawing lesson plan. Wonderfully puffy cumulus clouds floated on a soft breeze.

Our assignment, of course, was to draw and label. Not a bad way to spend an hour, even if you are an emotional wreck.

I settled into my chair, closed my eyes for just a minute, and fell into a reverie of daydreaming, or rather reenacting today's lunch-time scene, another meeting of the seventh-grade guys who were hoping to help me stay at GCA.

"We'll get work," Ray had said. He had waved his bologna and cheese sandwich in the air for emphasis.

"Work?" I had asked. "What kind of work?"

"We'll clean houses for old ladies," he said. "We'll wash cars. We'll mow lawns. We'll pick weeds. In short, we'll do what needs doing. We'll carry signs that say, *Will Work for Tuition*—"

"We will not!"

"Sorry," he said. "I got carried away. We'll—"

I didn't hear him. I'd already talked to mom about working my way through school.

"You're twelve, Stuart," she'd said. "Twelve is too young for that much responsibility."

"But—"

"No buts."

Ray's voice had warped me back to the lunch-time realities. "We'll have car washes on Saturdays at Arby's dad's gas station."

Hmm, I thought. That might actually be a plan.

A lot of agreeable sounds went around the circle.

"I'll ask," Arby had said.

But now, sitting in my lawn chair under the cloud-dotted sky, I wondered. I closed my eyes to think through each possibility. To try to think what Mom would say in response to each idea.

"Open up, Mr. Baltz."

"Oh, sorry, Mr. Hogan," I said. "Sorry."

"What's with the closed eyes?"

"Just thinking."

"Frogs again?"

I laughed. "No. School."

"Ah," he said. "I heard. So sorry, Stuart."

The way he said *Sorry* made me feel he really was distressed over my change of schools and that maybe he would find a way to pay my tuition himself. He didn't have any kids. Just his mom.

"I fully understand your predicament," he said.

"You do? Did this ever happen to you, Mr. Hogan?"

"Loss happens in different disguises. Change comes in a number of shapes."

Mr. Hogan crouched down beside my lawn chair.

"Stuart," he said, "it's going to be all right."

Did he mean he had worked things out with my mom and would be paying my way? Did he mean a bunch of the teachers, knowing that I was newly saved and not wanting me to go to a public school, had pooled their tax refunds to get me through school? Hope washed over me.

He laid a heavy, comforting hand on my shoulder. "How are you dealing with all of this? Are you trusting the Lord to keep you through any situation? Have you considered that the Lord might use you in the new environment?"

Ah. So, no plan from the teachers.

"Ray says he has a plan for us to work," I said, fumbling for something to say.

"Ray Sanchez?"

"Yes, sir. He thinks a bunch of us guys can make the tuition money."

"Hmm." Mr. Hogan looked up at the sky for a minute, like he was studying the clouds too. "It's my experience," he said, "that it's best to let parents make these specific types of decisions."

"But if it's just the money—"

"I'm only saying," he said, "and it's possible that I am not correct in this particular instance—but my experience in life would lead me to suspect that your mom has made a firm decision on this issue."

"Oh," I said. I felt heavy, weighed down in my lawn chair, like I might not be able to get up and run if someone yelled *fire*.

"So my advice for you is—not that you have asked my advice, of course—but my advice to you is that you accept your mom's decision. I am sure she considered all her options before choosing this particular one."

"She is really happy about it, actually. I guess that's my fault for hating this place for so long."

"Well, Stuart, your mom loves you very much." He spoke in a soft, gentle way, as if I were a hurt puppy. "I wish I had a videotape of her in the emergency room when you were hurt. You are her whole world, you know. You're all she has."

Naturally, I had never considered this.

"She's made the decision she thinks is right for you."

"If she were saved, she'd see that I need to be here," I said.

"Probably. But she isn't."

"So it's a vicissitude?"

"A definite vicissitude, Baltz." He got up. "Don't worry, Buddy," he said. "You'll be okay. You've been standing up for yourself for twelve years. Now you can stand up for Jesus."

I could have leaped tall buildings when he called me Buddy. I was ready to face the Hamilton hordes when he said "You'll be okay." But one question remained.

"Mr. Hogan," I said, "what's underneath when the floor caves in?"

"I beg your pardon?"

I shifted in my chair.

"Have you read *Sinners in the Hands of an Angry God*?"

"Of course."

"Well, under the unsaved person, there's hell, gaping at him like a starving monster."

"Yes?"

"What's under me? My world is falling apart too, but I'm saved." I wanted him to tell me that Romans eight twenty-eight was underneath, that everything would work out right, and that soon enough I'd be back here where I belonged.

"Underneath? You want to know what's underneath you when everything else crumbles?"

"Yes."

A faraway look lodged in Mr. Hogan's eyes. He stretched himself up to his full six-four and smiled in a way I could not interpret.

"Underneath, my friend," he said, "are the everlasting arms."

Then he shook his head slightly, as if to get ahold of himself, and smiled. "By the way, Mr. Baltz, I am personally acquainted with some young people who attend a Bible study at your new school. Get hooked up with them. They're good kids."

"Thank you, sir."

"Mr. Hogan!" A voice called from another part of the field. Mr. Hogan turned to leave, then turned back.

"Oh, and one more thing, Stuart—"

"Yes, sir?"

"Get those cloud drawings done and labeled. This is science class, remember?"

Lounging in my lawn chair, soaking up the early December sun, I sketched clouds and thought that maybe, just maybe, things were going to be all right after all.

19 Final Day

That night I ate forty-five deep-fried shrimp. Mr. Faladini threatened to charge me for them, but he kept them coming. Mom must have told him my life had been traumatic lately.

"You keep eating like that, boy, and I'm going to put you to work around here."

I laughed.

"I'm not kidding," he said. "A kid who can inhale that many shrimp can swab the deck around here, that's for sure."

"He's not working," Mom said with a laugh. "Better cut it out, Stuart, or Mr. Faladini will run out of shrimp."

"He'll work for me someday, count on it," said Mr. Faladini. "I have loaded this kid with so much shrimp, he will be drawn here involuntarily. I will employ this kid the minute he turns fourteen."

"Well," said Mom, "we'll see about that."

I wondered—thinking about working when I was fourteen—if I'd be able to come back to GCA for high school, if Mom and I would ever get a stucco house like the one I imagined, or if Hamilton Junior High School had a decent cross-country coach. I guessed I'd find out soon enough, at least about the cross-country coach.

It was Friday night. I'd lived through my final day at GCA, only cried a little bit when no one was looking, and went home empty-handed, except for my backpack which contained a treasure.

STUART'S RUN TO FAITH

All the seventh graders and the teachers had signed a giant Good-bye card for me. I'd had to fold it up to fit it in my backpack, but the minute I got home, I had unfolded it and devoured every word.

There were some trite phrases, such as *Have Fun at Hamilton,* and *Good Luck, Baltzman,* but there were others I read slowly, repeatedly, digesting every morsel.

> Dear Stuart,
>
> Before you came here, I thought I was a Christian, but after that discussion in Science, I realized I was only going along with the flow. I'm saved now.
>
> Thank you,
>
> Steven

And,

> Dear Stuart,
>
> Saturdays like always—decaf and weeding at Mr. Watson's house. Be there.
>
> Sincerely,
>
> Arby
>
> P. S. If Mr. Watson marries my grandma, you are NOT my uncle.

And,

> Dear Stuart,
>
> I will always remember how you and I stood against beginning a sentence with a preposition. I would have stood alone, but it relieved me to have you stand also. Maybe you can come back in high school.
>
> Your friend,
>
> Grace

It was almost worth leaving school to have *Your friend, Grace* written on a card I could get out and read every single day. I was sitting on the couch, reading my card over and over when Mom drove up.

"I'm on my dinner break," she said, "I came to get you—hey, what's wrong? Are you okay?"

It had finally caught up with me. I bawled like a baby.

"Is it the house?" she said.

"No. School." I am not a cry-er, and I felt stupid crying like a two year old who'd been told he couldn't have another cookie.

Mom seemed shocked, like she hadn't realized I was going to miss school.

"I thought you hated that school."

"Yes, but that was before."

"Before you took up Christianity?"

I nodded.

"I can't afford the house and the school bill," she said.

"I know." I wiped my eyes and felt stupid. "Sorry," I said. "It's okay." I was remembering what Mr. Hogan had said about me being Mom's whole life. For that, I could turn the faucets off and be a normal human person.

"Interested in some shrimp?"

"Absolutely."

So that's what brought me out to Cook's on Friday night with Mr. Faladini offering me a job the minute I could land a work permit.

Mom and I talked late that night. We talked about my running and my friends and school and her job and Grandma. And my dad.

"In a way, I guess I'm glad it's over," said Mom. "But not really."

"Me neither."

"With life, there's hope, as they say."

"Yeah."

"What does your Mr. Hogan say about it?" Mom asked.

He says God will work all of this out for my good and His own glory, and it might take years or maybe even my whole lifetime to understand how God works."

"Interesting," she said. "What else does he say?"

"He says you need to be saved." My heart was pounding. My mom's getting saved was the number one thing I wanted in the world, now that I'd met the Lord.

"I might just do that," she said. "Someday."

I fished my *Sinners* sermon out of my dresser later on and put it on the bookshelf where she'd be sure to see it. I asked the Lord to have her find it sometime when I wasn't home, so she could read it in peace and be scared out of her mind about hell like I was when nobody was around to make things all better. Nobody but Jesus.

20 Ms. Strong

Mom unloaded my bike from the back of the car after we'd done the paperwork for registering me at Hamilton. When she drove away, I stood there with my bike and waved after her. I walked my bike to the bike rack, locked it down, and hitched my backpack up onto my shoulder.

Okay, Baltz, I said to myself. *Here we go.* It was ten minutes till eight. Ten minutes to go. The secretary had pointed me in the direction of my first class, and I walked off that way, shoulders back, pretending this was my four hundredth day—not my first—at Hamilton Junior High School.

I'd spent my life in public schools before coming to Greenhaven Christian, but now that I was at Hamilton, I noticed a real difference. The difference was in *me.* Now that I was a Christian, things bothered me that wouldn't have bothered me before.

As I walked down the hall to my first class, I passed a group of kids talking. No problem. Kids can talk; what do I care? But when one of them took the Lord's name and spat it out in anger, I felt like I'd been shot. Then I saw three guys leaning against a wall, inhaling huge gulps of cigarette smoke and puffing out long streams of smoke. I choked down a laugh and hurried on to class. The reason I laughed was that I had the sudden realization that if that had happened at GCA, Mr. Thompson would have bounded out of his office like a gazelle and given those kids the lecture of their lives while hauling them bodily into his office to be expelled.

Most of the kids looked normal, of course—who wants to be weird?—but just before I arrived at room B-216, I passed a kid with a skull-and-crossbones tattooed on his cheek. That gave me the creeps, believe you me, and I was glad I had not ever done anything so indelible before I was saved. After all, sins wash off when a person trusts Christ, but tattoos—they're forever!

B-216 was English. And when the teacher said, "Class, today we'll be reviewing verbs," I sighed. Verbs, like nouns, was another third-grade concept that no one would ever—it seemed—give me credit for knowing. I wanted to shout "Verbs show action or state of being!" but probably people didn't shout at the teachers, even at this school.

I slunk through the day, hugging the walls, avoiding people. At lunch time, I tried to scope out a Bible study, but didn't see one. I ate my lunch alone.

Finally, it was two o'clock and time for the last class of the day: Life Science. I introduced myself to the teacher and hunkered down in the seat she told me to take. The teacher was a tall, gorgeous creature named Ms. Strong. She frightened and impressed me at the same time, and she was so beautiful I thought it might be worth coming to this school just to look at her. Then class started. And I got laughed at on my first day of school.

Ms. Strong took roll, introduced me to the class, and then began speaking in a soft, firm voice about Cro-Magnon man and Piltdown man, and a number of other fossil men and women who supposedly evolved from amoebas any number of millions of years ago. I spoke under my breath, but I guess Ms. Strong heard me.

"What was that, young man?" she said.

"I said God created the world out of nothing in six days." I had never been one to keep quiet, and being a Christian hadn't changed anything in that regard.

"Oh, we are a Creationist, are we?" said Ms. Strong with a sort of syrupy sweet voice pouring out on the pancake minds of her students.

"I'm a Christian, ma'am," I said, forgetting that at this school the kids probably didn't call their teachers "ma'am."

"Oh—Ma'am, is it?"

I tried to block out the rest of that embarrassing class. Ms. Strong couldn't plead her point with the scientific method—like Mr. Hogan had said—so she had to take to ridiculing my position. I just let her talk. I remembered Mr. Thompson saying, ". . . and respect the staff, even if you do not like them."

I rode my bike home and sang the second verse of my song.

Home, home, in the dumps

But at least I had friends and my Gram,

And now things are worse

And the kids at school curse

And the teacher evolved from an ape.

When I got home there was a message from Mom taped to the refrigerator: *I'll be late. Scrounge dinner. We'll shop tomorrow. Love, Mom.*

P. S. I'll be home by 9:00, I hope? Call me if you have trouble.

I opened the fridge but didn't see much in the way of dinner possibilities, so I closed the door and then stared around at the tiny house that was now the property of Baltz and Son.

I noticed the message light was flashing on our answering machine. I pushed the button.

"Stuart Baltz?" said an unfamiliar voice. "My name is Tradd Puckett. I go to Hamilton. We have a Bible study at lunch time for the Christian kids. It's on the West Lawn by the bike racks. I'll call you back later." Tradd's voice paused. "Good work in science, Stuart," he said.

There was another message.

"Hi, Honey. It's Grandma. I love you. Are you sure you won't come home again?"

And one more.

"Stuart—" and I knew this voice, "Hogan here. Calling to see how your first day went. I've been praying for you, and for your mom. I'll call you later. Bye."

I plopped down on my bed and threw my backpack in the corner of my room, and considered the day. What a loss. At least the phone calls from the Puckett kid and Mr. Hogan were encouraging. Still, all in all, I felt disjointed, abandoned. Lost.

All things work together for good flashed through my brain, but I tuned it out. It sounded too easy. Like no matter what happened to you, things would be hunky-dory. Like just getting good enough to run and be famous so your dad will love you. And then he dies. Or finally getting back to public school, and then the teacher makes fun of you on your first day. Or like when—

A car horn honked loudly in front of my house. I jumped up to see who it was.

"Mr. Watson!"

"Get in, Stuart," said Mr. Watson.

"Come on, Baltz," said Arby and Ray, crammed in the back seat, their laps piled with pizza boxes. "Hurry up before the pizza gets cold!"

I tried to be calm and nonchalant, but couldn't. I grinned an ear-to-ear smile and stuffed myself into the back seat.

"I already called your mom," Mr. Watson said. "She'll pick you up after work."

The feeling of being wrenched out of my own life melted away as I high-fived the guys and breathed in the healing smell of pepperoni pizza.

"Thanks, Mr. Watson," I said. "This is great."

"Not a problem," he said. "Not a problem."